Separate Hours

Other Books by Jonathan Baumbach

Separate Hours

a novel by

Jonathan Baumbach

 FICTION COLLECTIVE TWO

BOULDER • NORMAL • BROOKLYN

Published by Fiction Collective Two with
assistance from the New York State Council
on the Arts. Additional support given by
Illinois State University, the Publications
Center of the University of Colorado at
Boulder, Brooklyn College, and Teachers &
Writers Collaborative.

Address all inquiries to: Fiction Collective
Two, c/o English Department, Illinois State
University, Normal, IL 61761.

Baumbach, Jonathan,
    Separate Hours.

ISBN: 0-932511-28-7
ISBN: 0-932511-29-5

For A. G.

It is this part of the story that makes me saddest of all. For I ask myself unceasingly, my mind going round and round in a weary, baffled space of pain—what should these people have done? What, in the name of God, should they have done?

—Ford Maddox Ford,
The Good Soldier

There is a deception in amorous time (this deception is called: the love story).

—Roland Barthes
A Lover's Discourse

One

The Structure of Behavior

As a psychoanalyst, I am a profound believer in middles, in the life itself. Beginnings and ends are the stuff of fantasy. I once imagined that if I ever wrote the story of my life I would begin by saying, "Call me Shrink," a remark which offers the form of a joke without its substance and so disarms the reader by its foolishness. Someone so unguarded, someone toward whom you feel immediately superior, cannot be other than trustworthy. Watch out for me. I am full of tricks.

The aetiology of my condition was arrogance. I was, let me confess, overwhelmingly content with my life—with my career as analyst, with my brilliant and beautiful wife, with my precocious daughter, with my elegant West Side brownstone. I floated in the ether of contentment. Routine sustained me. So many hours a week of private practice, so many hours at the hospital, so many hours teaching a course at the university, so many hours with my family, so many hours writing my book. I was occupied from morning to night with matters of consequence. Let me say it now—it will come out soon enough—my wife Adrienne (my former wife Adrienne) is also a therapist. It gave us a common language, a common point of reference. I liked that, had come to it by premeditated choice. I had a companion with whom I could share the things that mattered, I thought, most to me. We had as good a marriage in our way, as intimate a friendship, as anyone we knew. We got along, didn't we? We got along famously, performed our roles with impressive conviction. I remind myself that this is the account of a man who saw only what it suited him to see. We had the appearance, the illusion, of a happy marriage.

In taking you into my confidence, I am playing a kind of confidence game. I want you to perceive me as a trustworthy witness, someone who will tell the truth even to his own disadvantage. My sanity has been thrown into question by Adrienne's opposing version of our shared reality. I leave it to you: which of us is unable to separate reality from wish. If one of us is telling the truth, the other, says reflex, is an extraordinarily persuasive lunatic. I begin with my first meeting with Adrienne.

I met Adrienne for the first time three different times.

one

I had a lunch date with a colleague and was picking him up at his office at the hospital. I was early, or he was late, and I camped out on a chair in his institutional waiting room. A tall elegant woman with large staring eyes came out of his office and gave me a corner-of-the-mouth smile. "I've kept the seat warm for you," she said.

two

I was lecturing on Transference at NYU, filling in for a friend, and Adrienne was in the audience, made her presence known by arriving a moment or so after I had begun. I was aware of her as if she was the only woman in the room and performed for her, rose to flights of eloquence usually beyond my range. She looked somewhat different from the woman I saw coming out of Ted Fieldstone's office—and I wasn't sure that she was the same person. I didn't get to talk to her after the lecture, though her aura lingered for me in the auditorium.

three

The occasion eludes me. It was a cocktail party, some official function of the Clinical Psychology Program. I was looking out a window, had my back to the party when someone said. "Yuri, I'd like you to meet the most talented student in the program." And there she was, the same striking woman, though sufficiently different to give me cause for wonder. We had an intense conversation of a kind usually only available to those who are likely never to see each other again or to analysand and analyst. She told me about problems in her marriage, about her childhood, about her anti-social obsessions, her tendency to outrageous behavior. And what did I reveal about myself? That I knew how to listen, that I was sympathetic. "I'll bet you're a very good therapist," she said. We were interrupted after about an hour by the presence of her husband, Ralph, who asked if she was ready to leave. Adrienne said no, to go without her if he was intent on going. Her tone was unequivocal yet gentle. Her answer angered him, though he pretended otherwise, remained willfully pleasant. How much longer would she be? he asked. She said in the same polite, slightly irritated voice that she had no idea, not to worry about her, she would manage to get home. As it turned out, the husband stayed on and they left together about midnight.

I've always thought it interesting how memories deform, how they're altered by revisionist feelings, the heart's betrayal of the past. I can witness the process in others, but I am unable to recognize it in myself—the desire to justify overwhelms the need to be true to oneself. I was connected to Adrienne from the start, was in love without naming it love. Adrienne seemed to me—do I actually remember

11

thinking that?—the woman that I was destined to spend my life with. The fact that she was already married seemed only a minor obstacle to be pushed aside. I realize how unfeeling this sounds, and I suspect I exaggerate to make my point, but it is a fair representation of the state of mind of my younger self. All behavior has its consequences—I would pay for my brutality in the end. I did not concern myself with the husband, did not concern myself with Adrienne's apparent lack of concern for him. If we were to be together, the husband had to be discarded. I accepted that necessity, taking no particular pleasure in the other man's pain. Mine was an infatuation that nurtured an already blooming arrogance. This way: if this wholly desirable woman desired me, I must be the remarkable man I imagined myself to be.

I didn't let things go by in those days. "What's the story with your marriage?" I asked from time to time. Her answer was usually evasive, a joke or a forlorn shrug. At the time I also had a wife, though we had not been living together for several months. I will come to that later, the implications of my first marriage. I have a weakness for digression—in some sense digression is everything—that I'll try to resist.

If this were a psychoanalytic paper, I might call it, "Marriage in an Age of Post-Civilization: Positives and Negatives." It took our subjects almost two years to get together after the couple's promising beginning. During this period of mock courtship, or more accurately mock marriage, A and Y's relationship fell into apparently irreparable disrepair any number of times. We're not talking about minor fights here, but actual break-ups, each avowing never to see the other again. Do damaged feelings ever really heal?

How many times did I swear to myself that I was through with her, that the woman was impossible? She was tense and high strung, vulnerable to changes of weather, her sense of well-being as fragile as spun glass. Let me cite examples. (I am a collector of evidence, an accountant of grievances.) At times we would contend over the meaning of an article in a magazine as if our existences were at stake. Neither of us could stand to be opposed by the other and yet it seemed as if we were always placing ourselves on opposite sides of an issue. When we held the same opinion, which was more often than either of us liked to admit, we tended to argue as to who held the opinion first. Am I making it sound worse than it was? Consider that I am remembering the past from the vantage of disenchantment.

I was crazy about her at her worst, particularly at her worst. I was enchanted with her.

Sometimes when we went to the movies we would get into a dispute about where to sit and end up sitting apart. More often than not I would make the necessary compromise and join her in the space she had chosen for us. I didn't recognize then that significant patterns in our relationship were defined in these seemingly trivial struggles. She was more absolute than I was, more vulnerable perhaps, so to keep the peace I tended to be the one to accommodate. I suspect I couldn't stand to have her favorable opinion—her respect, her affection, her love— withdrawn from me. I was addicted to her admiration, felt justified and rewarded by it, felt undeserving and in need, felt nurtured by it, felt anger at being in thrall to her. How many times did I give up on her in exasperation?

And then there was the matter of Adrienne's husband, Ralph, a lingering presence in our lives, the shadow behind our door. "Poor Ralph," as he was known in our private— our cruel— mythology. He had made a career out of having been a failed though promising student in an impressive variety of disciplines. He was the prodigal son as husband. There was nothing he couldn't do, said the myth, and nothing he ever completed. Adrienne supported him financially and emotionally, was reluctant to discard "poor Ralph" until he achieved self-sufficiency. This is the voice of self-interest and I apologize for its harshness. In truth, in unadmitted grievance, I was jealous of Ralph. Adrienne took a long time to leave him—for good, as we say—and I held Ralph responsible, an obvious displacement, for Adrienne's guilty procrastination. And maybe the ties between Adrienne and "poor Ralph" were more profound than I was willing to acknowledge. The son of a bitch had his ways. At some point, he became as much my problem as Adrienne's. We had extended conversations in bed, often immediately after love making, about what to do about Ralph. And what were we talking about, what was the real subject, when we talked about Ralph? Leave him, I wanted to say, though I generally took a less directive stance.

If only Ralph would throw me out, Adrienne would say in one vocabulary or another, if only he would stop loving me. I resisted asking why the decision rested with Ralph, assuming that we both knew, assuming mistakenly an understanding existed between us that transcended ordinary discourse. The assumption that we both traded on—I begrudgingly, Adrienne with apparent resignation—was that Ralph, an injured party, must be given the space to make his own decision. He really wants to be rid of me, Adrienne would say in her deep sexy voice, he just isn't ready to act on it yet.

While we waited for Ralph to achieve readiness, our intimacy deepened. We fought constantly. It was as if the integrity of our souls were at issue. I never fought with anyone as intensely as I fought with Adrienne during that period before our marriage that lasted actually three years but seemed to extend itself forever.

We were going off to a psychoanalytic conference in Boston together and had taken adjoining rooms in the same hotel. It was an opportunity, a rare one at that point, to spend an entire night together. I was to deliver a paper on transference, a work whose small clevernesses I imagined to be the flashes of light given off by genius. If I am being hard on my younger self, it is because he led me astray, set me up for a fall I was not prepared to take. I still recall the charge of

Adrienne's affection on the ride over, her sitting squeezed against me in our rented Dodge as though we were teenagers.

We sat in that rented Dodge Polaris, Adrienne's arm draped around my shoulders as if we were wearing each other like pieces of clothing. I had a hard-on for almost the entire trip from her proximity, from anticipation of our night together in the same bed. The exhilaration I felt scared me. I joked somewhat nervously as we rode like Siamese twins in that rented Dodge, made light of the conference, talked with false modesty about the implicit brilliance of my paper. I felt love for the woman next to me, felt the echoing intensity of her love for me, though I was afraid to break the spell by acknowledging the wonder of the moment with something as pedestrian as words. I assumed that my feelings—how powerful and articulate they seemed—spoke for themselves.

The weather changed radically as we neared Boston, an unseasonal blizzard resulting in an accident on the Mass. Pike, three cars and an enormous truck conspiring, which kept things at a standstill for over an hour. The snow piled up like a dunce cap on our hood. After the delay, there was barely time to check into our hotel rooms before the conference convened. The highway accident had made us both tense, reminding us how vulnerable we are to arbitrary circumstances. Adrienne seemed to blame me for the delay, for the hectic rush to the hotel along icy streets in poor visibility. I could see she was becoming irritated at my concern with being late. Yet she made no audible complaint. She wanted, as I did, our weekend together—all, everything—to be perfect.

After I gave the paper, after we had dinner with some other participants, after we had returned to my hotel room, we had a terrible fight. We were both on edge, Adrienne more intensely so. At some inevitable point, the ghost of Ralph appeared to fret us with its saintly claims. I said I thought we had agreed that Ralph was off-limits for the weekend. Then Adrienne announced that she wanted me to know—it had

15

been eating at her holding back the news—that she thought my paper was essentially "a tedious rehash of commonplaces." She had been terribly disappointed, having wanted so much to like what I had written. "To be frank," she said as if her previous unpleasantness had been a form of reticence, "to be frank, Yuri, I was really embarrassed when you read your paper, embarrassed as much for you as for myself. Why didn't you show it to me first? I would have told you to put it away."

I grumbled darkly, snarled, "I don't need you to tell me if what I do professionally is acceptable or not."

"Well, maybe you do," she said. "At least somebody should have had the grace to tell you not to give that paper."

I had my back to her, felt aggrieved though also defensive. "The conference committee was pleased with it," I said. "It couldn't possibly have been as bad as you say."

"It was both banal and dull," she said. "What worse!"

I did what I had to do, lifted her from the bed and carried her into the hall. She offered only token resistance.

"I don't ever want to see you again," she hissed through the closed door. "I mean it this time." I didn't doubt her.

Perhaps I had Scotch sent to my room or went down to the bar for a drink—it's as if this interval were vanished time— or went out into the snow for an aimless walk. Perhaps I tried to imagine my life—the next day, the day after— without this relentlessly painful relationship.

It was always when I had given up on her, when I hoped never to see her again, that she would return without apology and make amends.

There was a timid knock on the door at about two in the morning. It was as if I climbed out of my body—I was dozing, lying across the bed in my clothes—to arrive at the door. I considered not answering, I considered that the knock—really a tap—might have been a figment of a dream, though I answered the door before it repeated itself. She was standing there, huddled, childlike, smiling slyly, glancing away before I could catch her eye. "Are you still angry at me?" she asked in a voice barely meant to be heard. I made a gesture that suggested a variety of possibilities. Her smile apologized for itself. "Should I go away?" she asked.

"Yes, go away," I said. I put my arm around her waist and locked her against me.

She reminded me that the door to the hallway was open behind us, that someone, some secret agent of the respectable, might catch us in our illicit embrace. We were both at the moment fully clothed. I let go of her to close the door, still unreconciled. When I turned around she was lying on the bed in provocative pose. "Do you want to fuck, doctor?" she whispered in mock-German accent, an imitation of one of my imitations.

"You think you're irresistible, don't you," I said, angry at myself for being so readily charmed.

I remember the fierceness of our lovemaking if not the specifics. I remember the desire and terror, the exchange of orgasms like the taking of vows. We had sex several times during that long night as if fucking or sucking was the appropriate language of forgiveness, the only undeniable proof.

We had proven to each other that we could survive the unforgivable.

On the drive back—much of this account is of comings and goings—I said lightly, lightly treading air, "I'm sorry you hated my paper, sweetheart."

She looked at me—I watched her from the corner of my eye as I drove—with unaffected surprise. "You don't really believe that, do you? I can't imagine that you really believe that, Yuri. You know better, don't you? I say a lot of things I don't mean. You know I respect you a lot."

I only knew it when she told me it was so. It's possible that I misread her all along, had been willing to believe whatever flattered me and deny the implications of the rest.

I am skipping ahead, pursuing some private chronology of Significant Events. I was at a Psychology Department party, an end of term spiked-punch affair. The chairman, who was no friend of mind, got me into a corner to discuss ostensibly— I have some theories about his motives but will not pursue them here—marginal Ph.D candidates. Adrienne's name came up. I don't know that he knew we were living together, but he had to know there was some tie between us. Still, he proceeded to talk about her with unconcealed dislike. "The woman is a snakepit," he said. "She should never have been allowed to remain in the program."

I made an awkward attempt to defend her, presuming she needed no defense, mentioned how perceptive she was, how finely tuned, how smart. It was not a conversation I needed, though a difficult one to escape. I was a part-time faculty, dependent on the chairman's good graces for my employment.

"*Entre nous*, this lady's trouble," he said. "I happen to know there's serious disturbance there."

There was more. Was I betraying her by continuing to listen to him? He was talking about Adrienne using her seductiveness in her dealings with men when I found some excuse to leave the party.

At first I wasn't going to mention this conversation to Adrienne, but then I decided—I worried the issue until it clarified—that silence was a form of betrayal, a way of feeling superior. Still, I muted Norman's malice in reporting his remarks. Even in the diluted form I gave them, they precipitated a fight. The bearer of bad news never gets off easily.

"Norman is a malicious fool," I repeated over and again. "No one takes Norman seriously."

"What you refuse to see," she said in the voice of superior wisdom. "is that what went on between you and Norman has more to do with you than with me."

I could read her mood well enough to see what was

coming and took her hand, which she let me hold only long enough to feel its loss when it was gone. My objective was to forestall the inevitable.

"I'm very upset," she reminded me.

"I understand that," I said. "It's upsetting to find out someone is whispering malice about you."

She stared at me with undisguised dislike. "Why are you doing this to me?" she asked.

"Doing what, sweetheart?" I strove to be reasonable.

"If you don't know," she said as if she were offering privileged information to someone without the appropriate clearance, "you're much more limited than I thought. I really don't see how you can be a therapist and be so blind to your own motives."

"You're the only one that matters to me in this," I said, distrusting the assertion as I made it, raising my voice.

"I hate it when you scream at me," she said. "It makes me hate you."

"I'm not your enemy," I said in the voice of an already engaged combatant. "If I withheld Norman's viciousness to protect your feelings, that would be patronizing. Norman is an asshole. I suspect that he was attracted to you and felt put down at not getting what he wanted."

"I slept with Norman," she said, turning her face away.

The news had too much impact to allow it to register.

"Why are you saying that?" I think I said.

She took my hand, was unusually solemn. "I'm not making it up, Yuri."

"When was this?"

"It was before I knew you," she said. "I was in training analysis with him." She squeezed my hand as an offer of reassurance. "I didn't stay with him for long."

"Whose idea was it?" I asked.

She averted her face, said nothing I could hear.

I fantasized exposing Norman's treachery, though realized there was nothing I could do. "I'd like to break him in half," I said.

I don't remember where we were—what room, which place— when this confrontation took place. Adrienne was sitting next to me, impacted, suffering, her hand on my hand. I was torn between revulsion and tenderness, left her for another room, then found my way back, impelled to heal the rift between us.

I omit the silences in this account.

"Norman doesn't matter to you," Adrienne said. "You really want to kill me." She had her head turned away when she made this pronouncement so I had no way of reading her face.

I muttered something about the abuse of authority, though I recognized that Adrienne was right or mostly right or partly right. I asked her why it had happened.

"No reason," she said. "Self-loathing maybe."

"You're too good for that," I said.

She laughed. "That's the voice of love speaking," she said.

I realize how selective this document is, how much of consequence it leaves out. The claims of feeling, in their moment, seem to drive out all else. One tends to fall in love with those to whom the psychological prophesies of childhood lead. We were fighting to free ourselves from an inescapable emotional destiny. If our love couldn't survive disappointment and betrayal and violent battles of will, what was the point, whispered mock-logic, in continuing together?

I've mentioned Adrienne's problems in freeing herself from Ralph's dependency, though I have mentioned nothing of the difficulty in dissolving my marriage to Patricia. Aggrieved by my defection, Patricia had refused to give me a divorce. Gradually her position had moderated and we had been negotiating through lawyers—and occasionally by phone directly—a closure to our marriage. So when she suggested that we meet and talk in person about a settlement I consented despite Adrienne's objection to my going. Adrienne's resistance to the meeting became more impassioned as the time for the appointment neared.

The meeting with Patricia is not in itself the issue here, is of less concern than Adrienne's opposition to my having a drink in public with a woman I had been estranged from for over two years. At the time I thought the issue was jealousy, which I found both flattering and upsetting. It was more likely that Adrienne didn't want our situation to change, needed the frisson of ghostly shadows sharing our bed. The powerful factor of the illicit.

But also of course it was a test, her asking me not to go, the kind of test I could only hope to fail. If I didn't accede to her wishes, it proved that I didn't love her. If I did give in, I proved myself easily controlled and so unworthy of her respect.

I arrived at the lounge of the Royalton Hotel, ten minutes late for our appointment, changed my seat three times waiting for Patricia to make her belated appearance. When I saw her come in the door wearing a white blouse and light blue skirt, I remembered having loved her. The feeling was unexpected, almost shocking, given my indifference toward her for the longest time. There was something bridelike in her appearance. She blushed when she sat down across from me in the booth, a compelling illusion. I felt a kind of longing and it struck me that Adrienne had an intuition about what would happen, that she knew me in a way I didn't know myself. Still, I pursued my errand in a businesslike way, said it made little sense after all this time not to get a divorce. I anticipated resistance and got none. Patricia said—it was as if I had dreamed her remarks—that she saw no point in being tied to a man who was no longer her husband. We were for the first time in years in agreement. She had the signed papers with her and took them out of her purse. I felt relief and a sense of loss, thought how pleased and surprised Adrienne would be. Appreciative of Patricia's grace, I ordered champagne to celebrate the waning moments of our marriage. We toasted each other's future, then sat with nothing to say to each other, our business concluded. I was feeling a little sad, holding on to the moment of our last goodbye, when Patricia mentioned that she had taken a room in the hotel that seemed a pity not to use.

I didn't get home until late. Adrienne, who was in bed reading as it turned out, contrived to ignore my entrance. I sensed that I was in for trouble.

We were living in four small rooms at this point—a floorthrough in a brownstone—the kitchen as narrow as a finger. I was making myself a drink in the narrow kitchen when Adrienne came up behind me. I wasn't aware of her until she spoke. "How did it go?" she asked.

I took the signed agreement from the breast pocket of my jacket and passed it to her without turning around.

"That's unexpected," she said, then put her arms around me from behind. I tensed self-protectively, ducked my head. She laughed. "You act like a man with a bad conscience."

I admitted to nothing, took my drink into another room— perhaps left the kitchen without it. Adrienne followed. I yawned, said I thought I'd go to bed, steeled myself against an accusation she refrained from making.

We stayed up the remainder of the night talking about other things, case studies, the marriages of friends, regression, transference, fears of dying. The apparent subject, we were trained to know, was almost never the real subject.

Was it a mistake not to acknowledge that I had slept with Patricia that evening, not in exchange for a divorce, nothing as crude as that, but to pursue the illusion of connection one last time? Adrienne knew of course and I knew she knew. There was that between us.

There are a few more incidents to be covered—fragments of evidence—before I get to the present.

This comes back to me: I was at the airport with Adrienne's sister Grace, who had come to New York for our wedding and was now returning to her guru in Denver. Her flight was delayed for an hour and we went to the cocktail lounge for a drink. Grace had difficulty deciding what to order and I was struck by that, the similarity between sisters, the use of tentativeness as a form of control.

"I am really glad that you and Adrienne got together," I remember her saying. She ordered a Bloody Mary, then changed her mind and switched to grapefruit juice. It was something she had said before, the comment about our getting together, something she seemed pleased to repeat.

"We're unexpectedly alike, Adrienne and I," I said. "Superficially different yet unexpectedly alike."

"That's like the opposite of what I was going to say," Grace said. "I was thinking really how totally different the two of you are. Adrienne likes things just so. Nothing has ever been good enough for her. Know what I mean?"

I said yes, then no not exactly, wanting to hear how it seemed to Grace.

"I think Adrienne idealizes you," she said. "Do you mind if I have another juice?"

I ordered a drink for me and a juice for Grace. "Adrienne sees into my every fault," I said.

Grace shook her head in her solemn way. "That's not the way she talks about you to me."

"What does she say about me?"

Grace rebuked my curiosity with a shocked stare. She whispered her answer or rather mouthed the words so I wasn't sure what I heard. "She thinks you're wonderful," she might have said. I had the impression Grace was blushing. It was the only time I'd seen her show embarrassment.

"I didn't get that," I said.

Grace seemed amused at my request to repeat her confidence, said she thought I had heard her perfectly well.

"You have a way of confiding and withholding at the same time," I said. "One has to lean forward to hear you, has to read your lips."

"But not my heart," she whispered, offering her words and taking them back. "Look, Yuri, whatever you do, try not to disillusion her. Okay?"

"It's unavoidable," I said. I noted that it was time for her to go to the boarding gate.

"That makes me very sad," she purred as we left the bar, the reference already elusive. "It really does. There must be something you can do to avoid it."

What I could do, what I did in fact, was to pretend not to understand her.

What is missing from my account is the texture of our life together, the dailiness, the habits of routine, the major and minor pleasures. I think of this memoir as a rational inquiry into the mysterious.

When the passion became domesticated, when it no longer seemed a matter of life and death to make love, we were easier with each other for awhile, more protective and affectionate. I don't know if that's true. What is true? The urgency went away but not far, came back like a recurring dream, was always there.

The following fragments are from a journal I've kept on and off over the years. It's in my handwriting so that I know that it's mine but I don't remember having written it.

When Rebecca feeds at Adrienne's breast alongside me in bed, I am jealous of them both. They exclude me and it is painful to be left out. . . . Adrienne lets me taste her milk. She cups my head from behind as I drink. The birth of the child has made her motherly to almost everyone. Do her patients notice the difference? In the office we share I can smell the aura of her milk. . . . We argue over who will take Rebecca to her first day of school. No serious argument. We take her together, one on each side, our hands connecting us. At school, Adrienne can't bear to separate, has to steal herself to leave. I am there to tear her loose. Rebecca herself is more matter of fact, lets her parents carry the brunt of her anxiety at separation. . . . I never thought I would say this to myself— much of my childhood spent resisting the urge to cry—I am a happy man, a happy happy man.

Every day, excluding Sunday, for much of every day, I talked to people who were in some kind of pain, their lives deformed, their senses of self incompletely or negligibly defined. Professionalism aside, I would have had to be absolutely heartless not to carry some of it away, I imagine it was the same for Adrienne, though it was a subject—one of many—we tended to avoid. I was made continually aware of how fragile human transactions are, how dangerous intimacy can be, how one never fully escapes the configurative relationships of childhood. Self-destructive patterns asserted themselves after years of apparent remission. Long term relationships went abruptly bad at some predictable point as if fulfilling an inexorable destiny. Sex staled. Affection dissipated. Couples turned one another through a kind of compulsive alchemy into false unloving parents.

Sooner or later, said the evidence of my patients' lives, relationships were bound to fail. It was a constant warning to me not to let things slide in my own marriage. I came to believe that marriages like individual lives had to be continually reinvented, that they survived the loss of romance only as a matter of will. Those who couldn't or wouldn't will that survival came apart, sought love elsewhere, came to hate one another. We were the exceptions. We tended the fire. Whenever I reflected on it, I thought how enduring our marriage was, how intimate, how full of affection and respect. The worst had come and gone before we even started out.

Therapists are not necessarily less susceptible to delusion than people in other professions.

Sometimes in watching the slow-motion replay of a disastrous moment in a baseball game, I feel myself willing the event altered in its recurrence. It is a magical, contrary to fact hope, a commitment to unreality, an unwillingness to accept loss and, ultimately, death. It is the same for me in telling this story.

Two

The Divided Self

Bear with me. Words tend to hide in my throat. Sometimes I am at a loss for words.

We are having dinner. We are almost finished with dinner. Rebecca, who is eight (ate), asks if she can be excused. Yuri looks at her plate with his accountant's eye. "You haven't eaten very much, honey," he says.

"Oh let her go," I say. "She's eaten as much as she wants."

Yuri scowls. "Bec," he says, "one more piece of meat and you're a free woman." Rebecca, wanting to please, stuffs down two pieces for her daddy. When she gets up, I hold out my arms to her. She gives me a hug (and Yuri a kiss) and goes her way.

"I didn't mean to undermine you," I say. "I just wanted to talk to you about something not for Rebecca's ears."

He gives a sigh of exasperation. "If you had made the decision first, I would have gone along with it."

"I know you would," I say. I come over and put my arms around him. "Do you want to hear about this wild man Peter sent to me as a referral?"

"What wild man? You're not talking about Brian Carroway by any chance?"

"How do you know about him?"

"I was the one who sent him to Peter. I diagnosed him over the phone as a borderline sociopath."

"That's sort of glib, isn't it? What does that mean, borderline sociopath? If someone else used the term, you'd find it offensive. How can you diagnose someone over the phone?"

"Come off it, Adrienne," he says, smiling as if it were a game we were playing. "So what do you want to tell me about Brian Carroway? You're having some problem with him or you wouldn't have brought him up."

I tell him what I can, what I think he wants to hear. I tell him about Carroway's assaultive manner, about his graphic sexual confessions, about his coming on to me, but not that he has an astonishing face. I make him sound (it is the way words play tricks on meaning) worse than I think he is.

"It sounds to me as if he's using the therapeutic situation as an occasion for exhibiting himself," Yuri says in his measured way. "If he makes you uncomfortable, I'd say drop him. Not everyone can be helped. Why make life more difficult than it has to be?"

I am tempted to argue, though I resist that particular temptation. I am tempted to say that maybe I can do something for him where you and Peter can't. "I'll have to sleep on it," I say. "I can't come to decisions as quickly as you can."

He puts his arm around me (we are sitting on the brown velvet loveseat with the tear in the back) and he says, "I only told you what you wanted to hear, A. I could tell from the way you told the story what your decision had been."

Sometimes I like that. That he has to prove to me how smart he is. "I like that you watch over me," I say.

My first take when he strutted into my office that November afternoon was that this man was arrogant and narcissistic, possibly dangerous. (What I meant by dangerous I didn't know at the time.) His manner was terribly solemn. I was aware in the most intense way of the nervousness he made small effort to repress. The astonishing beauty of his face repelled me. I felt assaulted by the aggressive insistence of his presence.

He was unexpectedly shy. Spoke haltingly at first. Carroway (as he called himself) was thirty-six, a real estate broker, former newspaperman, former free-lance publicist. He had a wife named Anna Marie, who was a dancer. No children. His wife, he said, had been in the chorus line of two failed Broadway musicals. When I asked which ones, he said he couldn't remember the names. (He didn't inspire trust.)

The preliminaries out of the way, we sat facing each other, chair to chair, and I asked as I do, "How have you been?"

He shrugged. "I have to get this off my chest," he said. "You're not what I pictured. You're super-attractive for someone in your line of work."

My heart fluttered. "That's uncalled for, Carroway," I said. "I wasn't just saying that as a come on," he said. "You really have amazing eyes."

I gave him my severest look. (I hated his crudeness.) "You don't have to seduce me to enlist my sympathy," I said.

He hung his head in parody of a scolded child. "No one wants to hear the truth," he said under his breath. "If I offended you, doctor, I assure you it wasn't my intention."

"I understood from Dr. Konig that you were having marital problems," I said. "I think we ought to talk about why you're here."

His manner remained languid, though his attention was unwavering. He had the quality (studied, I suspected) of making you feel that you were the only person in the world that interested him. "I'm not so to speak my own problem," he said. "I am and I'm not, if you know what I mean. I believe if you hear me out, you'll see that my situation doesn't fit into any preconception."

"No one's does," I said. "I make no preconceptions."

"I like that you say that," he said. "Anna Marie and I

have what I believe is called an open marriage. Okay? It's not for everyone, but it's worked for us. We take our fun, so to speak, where we find it." He winked at me.

I began to dislike him more and more. "I've had other patients with open marriages," I said. (Is that true? I wondered.)

"Have you?" He gave me an unhappy smile. "Marriage, Dr. Tipton, is just a convenience in my opinion, a useful arrangement. Why should we cut ourselves off from other pleasurable relationships merely because we have a wife or a husband. Do you see what I'm saying?"

"You don't have to sell me on your life style," I said. "I'm capable of appreciating its value to you without finding it desirable for myself."

He established eye contact. "Maybe you're missing something," he said.

"You're behavior is inappropriate," I said. "Maybe that's your problem, Carroway."

He held up both hands in a mock-gesture of surrender. "Okay." He took a deep breath, smiled his insinuating smile. "I have this thing going with a waitress at the Holiday Inn in Port Washington. We get it together twice a week either in my car or hers. Okay? When in my car I sit behind the wheel and she bellies down on the passenger seat and she—I hope this doesn't embarrass you—she like takes my prick in her mouth. In her car, we reverse the procedure. She gets behind the wheel and I stick my head under her apron—I really get off on the apron—and I like make a meal of her. That's the drill. My car or yours?"

"Excuse me," I said. (I felt assaulted by his story. Couldn't believe for a while I was hearing what I heard.) "I don't see the point."

"The point?" He laughed obscenely. "This is the point. "When we got into bed for the night, I would describe the experience to Anna Marie, blow by blow so to speak. That was when things were still good between us. In turn, Anna

Marie would tell me everything she'd been up to that day in the sexual arena. We thought of it as a kind of sharing."

My palms were sweating. (I was in a minor panic.) "This was regular practice between you?" I said, less question than a summing up. "You had promiscuous extra-marital relations, which you tended to confide to each other."

"That's on the mark," he said. "On Fridays during my lunch hour, there's this rich woman, a former client, who stops by for me at my office. She picks me up in her white Mercedes and takes me to this motel in Great Neck for a quick hit. That's been going on for almost two years. I think of it as business as usual. The woman likes to be roughed up, which is not the way I operate. Also she's older than me and she's losing her looks. Why am I telling you this? I lost my train of thought here." He caught me glancing at my watch. (Fifteen minutes to go.) "Am I boring you?" he asked.

"I feel mistreated by you," I said. "You're hostile and you're an exhibitionist. Will you please get to the point?"

"I know what you're saying, Dr. Tipton, but that's the way we live our lives," he said, smiling faintly. "I mean, hey we go for the gusto. This is the point. About a month ago, Anna Marie started to freeze me out. Do you know what I'm saying? She froze me out on the good stuff. She began to hold things back or tell me stories I could tell were not true."

"Did you ask her her reasons for the change?"

He held his head in his hands. He dramatized suffering. "She said things like, 'It isn't worth talking about?' If she had to keep it secret, it was like more important to her than what we had."

"Did she cut off sexual relations with you?"

"You're very perceptive, doctor." He flashed me his soulful look. "Actually, she never stopped making it with me, but some of the fire, so to speak, was gone."

"What fire is that?" I asked.

He started to say something in the same impassive manner, then he stopped himself and he got to his feet. "This

31

isn't funny to me," he said. His face was flushed with anger. "This is my life."

I rejected the impulse to apologize. "I don't really want to see you again," I said.

His smile had a reptilian aspect. "Is that a professional decision, Dr. Tipton?"

"Yes, it's a professional decision," I said. (I couldn't believe how much I disliked him.) "I can make referrals. I usually don't turn patients away, but I can see we're not right for each other."

"Are you afraid of me?" he asked. "Is that the problem?"

"Of course not." I met his aggressive stare out front. (I *was* afraid of him. I had fantasies of shouting for help if he made the slightest move toward me.) "I think you're a narcissist, Mr. Carroway. I think you've come to see me as an occasion to undress verbally." I stumbled on the last word, say "versually."

"I've been under stress," he said, sitting down. "I'm not like this all the time."

"I trust my intuitions," I said, looking at my watch. (There is a clock on the wall which I tend to ignore.) "That's all the time we have. We've run ten minutes over."

"If you won't see me as a patient, will you see me on other terms?"

"No chance."

"It's good that you don't take any crap from me," he said. "I like that. I like the way you handle yourself."

The decision came to me before I came to it. "I'll see you one more time," I said.

He had a look of gratitude on his amazing face. I felt pleased oddly to have pleased him. We made an appointment for the following Friday at the same time.

The weight of his absence when he left troubled me.

In the early years of my marriage, I used to get anxiety attacks in which I felt I couldn't breathe. It was like some enchantment came over me. I just couldn't catch my breath. Once I almost passed out on a subway platform. A motherly black woman took me by the arm and led me into the air. Held me up (in air) until I could breathe again. If she would have adopted me, I remember saying to Yuri, if she would marry me, all my problems would be solved. I tended to discuss everything with Yuri then. I couldn't make decisions without his advice. I hadn't learned to trust my intuitions. It wasn't that my self-esteem was low. It was just that I trusted Yuri's judgments above my own. (I was full of self-doubts.) Yuri's sureness seemed to me something near miraculous. A problem to be solved? Yuri knew the answer even before the question had been fully asked.

For the longest time, I trusted Yuri's judgments over my own. It had to do of course (I say of course, though it is a new discovery for me) with my being a woman. For years I brought my difficult cases to Yuri as if he were a higher court of opinion. What I began to do was to solicit his opinion only to take the opposite tack. I had to have my own way to be myself.

Yuri also relied on me. He needed me to confirm him. I was there to admire the wisdom of his judgments. It was my role (my job) to give him back his own opinion as if it were also mine. I didn't mind. When Yuri didn't get what he wanted from me (I couldn't always be his echo), he would struggle against my opinion as if it were crushing him under its weight. So much power scared me. I couldn't ever advise him; he didn't really want my advice. And then I no longer wanted his. (This has been a secret from ourselves.) We continued out of habit (continued and continue) to offer each other advice.

Carroway swoops in ten minutes late, silk shirt open almost to the navel, leather jacket over his shoulders. What timing! I had just about given up expecting him. The frisson of something unacceptable is in the air between us. He sits back in his chair and makes a point of crossing his legs. Makes a point of looking me over.

I am the one in charge, I tell myself. "How are you today?" I ask.

"I read somewhere that jealousy is the most humiliating of emotions," he says. "The most destructive of all human feelings. I am living testimony to that."

"What are you jealous of exactly?"

He looks down at his elegant hands, unsuccessfully conceals a smile. "I am jealous of every man who has a desirable woman that is not available to me. Your husband, as a matter of fact."

"You're jealous of my husband? That's not really true, is it?" (My voice is like a cool breeze.) "I'm still not clear why you've come to see me, Carroway. What are you looking for really?"

"Peace of mind," he says. "Okay? Look, I make good money. This last year, knock wood, has been terrific. I have a super-nice house with spacious grounds, a sauna, a pool room, an attack dog, a view of the sound. I'm like laying out my jewels before you, Adrienne." (He mispronounces my name.) "And I have a beautiful wife—it is not my opinion alone. A lot of men would like to be in my pants, so to speak. Why aren't I satisfied?"

"You tell me."

He closes his eyes. "Okay. I'm unsatisfied because my wife is driving me crazy."

"Yes?"

"Anna Marie loathes and despises me," he says. "I have stood in the way of her growth and development as a person."

"She has told you this in so many words?" (My question seems to puzzle him.)

He shakes his head. "She said to me last night that the

34

reason for her freezing me out is to keep herself from going crazy. I like don't see it frankly. I never asked from her anything I wasn't willing to give myself."

"That doesn't mean it was what she wanted," I hear myself say. "Does it?"

He turns his attention on me. He gives me the full light of his interest and regard. "That's right on the money," he says. "So when I say to her I don't see what her problem is, she says, 'I suppose you expect me to do what your waitress does or that little woman in the bookshop or that nude model or the wife of that assemblyman.' I told her I didn't want her to do anything she didn't want to do. 'Fine,' she says, and she disappears into the bathroom. She returns in this abbreviated red lace nightgown. 'I want to be eaten,' she says to me, 'like a banquet.'"

(I sense that he is reading my face. What is he looking for?)

"You don't want to hear this, right?" he says, offering me his sad (his post-coital) smile. "If you want me to stop, just say the word."

"Well," I say, laughing nervously. "What you're talking about now seems relevant to your problem. There's a difference, isn't there? Look, I'm not a prude."

"I don't want to offend you, Dr. Tipton," he says, using the name as if it were a private joke between us. "But like it or not, my life is my life. Do I continue?" (I nod reluctantly.) "So I say to Anna Marie, 'I'm not interested, baby. I don't have to do anything I don't want to do either.' A little later, I do exactly what she asked, but I go down on her not because she demanded it—do you see what I'm saying?—but for myself. In the middle of things, so to speak, the bitch starts screaming at me."

The man is describing oral sex with his wife and my mind begins to wander. (Why don't I ever get what I want? I think. Don't I deserve as much as Anna Marie?)

"She is like screaming her head off, 'You're not doing it

right, Carroway. You don't love me.' 'That's a fucking lie,' I say. 'You lie so much you wouldn't know the truth if it bit you.' 'I'm sorry, babe,' she says. 'Finish me.' After she comes she says, 'I hate you, Carroway. I really hate you.' Does that make any sense?"

"Did you ask her what was going on with her?" I ask.

"You kidding me?" he says. "Anna Marie has a fifteen word vocabulary."

"Did you even try to discuss it with her?"

He lifts his head as if pulling it away from the flower of his wife's sex. "As a rule," he says, "I don't make gestures that are not fully acceptable."

"I don't understand what you're saying."

"Look, I know you're super smart," he says. "What I'm saying, let me put this as well as I can, what I'm saying is that I make it a point of honor never to go any place I'm not desired. Do you get what I mean? It's not important."

"What I hear you saying, Carroway, is that you anticipate what the other person wants. You do what you know will ingratiate you. That's manipulative. It's also very passive."

He stifles a yawn. "Now you're losing me, Dr. Tipton," he says. "I have a question for you. Would you carry a message for me to the other Dr. Tipton? Would you tell him that Carroway envies him his wife?"

(Basking in his narcissistic light as if he were carrying me into that private mirror in which he lives.) "Do you flatter everyone you want something from?" I ask him. "Is that the way you get what you want from the world?"

"I always speak from the heart," he says. "Sometimes I lie a little. You've seen right through me from the start. You know that."

"I don't know," I say. "What have I seen?"

"My flaws of character," he says, leaning forward as if he means to offer them to me. "I want to say that you're very good at what you do."

"And you're incorrigible," I say. (Does he know the

affect he has on me? He is more complicated than he lets on.) "I still don't know what you need me for." (The remark is infelicitous.) "Carroway, your marital difficulties may be an outgrowth of the pressure you put on your marriage. I'm talking about your sexual arrangements. Infidelity, even by agreement, can erode the conditions that keep people together. The two of you have been playing with erotic fire and now you've gotten burned. It's...."

He interrupts. "I want to continue seeing you," he says, more like a lover than a patient. "Don't cut me off."

"I'm not sure I'm the right therapist for you," I say. "You know all too well how to get around women."

"I don't seem to be getting around you," he says. "So, where do we go from here, Adrienne? You want to see me again or what?"

"I have to think about it," I say. "We could have another exploratory session, Carroway, and end it there. Or I could give you the names of some other therapists who I think you would get on with."

He reads me under that piercing light of his. "Why do you think you're not the person for me?" he asks. (Of all things: he is watching his performance through my eyes.)

"I don't even know that I have any hours open for you next week," I say, not sure what I want. "Why don't you call me tomorrow at five and I'll let you know." (I can barely catch my breath.)

"I can survive without you," he says.

"I may have a cancellation. Call me tomorrow between four and five, why don't you?" My manner is as businesslike as panic allows.

He gets up from his chair as though it were giving birth to him. "Thank you for your trouble, Dr. Tipton," he says, holding out his hand.

"We'll talk," I say, avoiding his hand, his touch, his face. Endangered by something unseen.

"I don't know if I'll call," he says.

(He is rejecting me. How wonderful!) "Then I'll expect your call or I won't," I say.

His exit is managed without the calculated poise of his entrance. It is a relief, I tell myself, to have him out of my hair. (Which hair? Witch hair.)

We meet halfway on the basement stairs, Yuri coming down as I ascend. I throw him a kiss, which he takes as his due. He points his index finger at me. Bang bang.

I feel emptied out. I take two Tylenol caplets and lie down. I put my hand on my heart. (It may not even be where I think it is.) I listen to myself breathe.

I wake to a kiss between the eyes. Yuri says, leaning over me, "What are we going to do about dinner?"

I wake in an erotic phase. Why don't you just eat me like a banquet, I think of saying. This familiar man, sitting half-turned away on the bed, is talking of taking Chinese food in for dinner, has General Tso's chicken on his mind. I touch his arm. I rub it as if it were a magic lamp. Otherness is an unbridgeable distance. (When we met he told me he was five ten; I said I was five seven and a half. One day last month, I realized we were really the same height.)

"Do we have a date for tonight?" he asks.

"Why don't you make the decision about dinner?" I say. "I don't want to think about it."

Two things upset me today. Two trifles. A letter from an insurance company addressed to Dr. and Mrs. Tipton. Yuri showing me a rather charming love note from one of his clinical psych students.

"Does it tempt you?" I ask. He insists not. But he says, only partly joking, "She's a major temptation. If I were a free man, I don't know what I'd do."

We joke about it back it forth, which brings on a kind of panic. (Am I jealous? If so, of which one?) I can't leave well enough alone. "Have you thought of not discouraging her?" I feel compelled to ask. "Don't you think that possibility should also be explored?"

The desirable psychologist grins foolishly. "She has this slutty quality which I find very appealing," he says. "She's looks a bit like the actress—I can't remember her name—in "Last Tango in Paris."

"Yuri, why don't you take her up on her offer if she's so appealing?" I hear myself say. "What's stopping you?"

"You know what stops me," he says. His face shows that I have wounded him.

"You don't like to take risks, do you?" I say. "You don't go after what you want and then you act as if it's my fault."

"There are things I value that I don't want to lose," he says.

The moment his assertion moves me, I feel myself distrust it. "That's your excuse, honey," I say. "You can't have something unless you're also willing not to have it."

We have a fight that never quite takes place. Yuri wears his misunderstood look like a prize through dinner. I recall in the evening that Carroway hasn't phoned for an appointment. My take is, that his defection (rejection?) may be the source of my irritation with Yuri. I apologize for my bitchiness. (It's hard for me to say I'm sorry and mean it. It always feels like an obligation.)

When I come to bed, Yuri reaches for me. It is a gesture that evades the anger he must be feeling. I say the first thing that comes to mind. "I want you to eat me like a banquet."

"My pleasure," he says and he slides his head under the covers into the regions of the night.

Three

The Psychopathology of Everyday Life

Two summers ago on Martha's Vineyard—we have a small summer house in Chilmark—Adrienne took up sketching, did a series of drawings of seagulls in flight. Almost every morning she would sit on a desk chair on the screened-in porch that overlooked the ocean and absorb herself in private vision. She sketched while I went through the motions of writing my book on counter-transference, a subject I had been pursuing for some time with a diminishing sense of obligation. Sandy, the teenaged girl we had brought with us from the city, would take Rebecca, who was eight that summer, for a walk on the beach while we worked. When concentration failed me as it did too often that summer, I would watch Adrienne from my window, her impassive face like a bird's, sketching on an oversized pad I didn't know she owned. I thought of it as a way of locking herself out of the world, a way of justifying through worked-up occasion her need to withdraw. The withdrawal, not the sketching, concerned me. I missed her. The Adrienne I knew, presumed to know, was missing.

I tried to involve myself in her activity, asked to look at her drawings, pointed out the ones I liked, but she knew that my interest was contrived. "You don't have to say anything," she said. "They're nothing in particular."

"Why do you do them if they're nothing?" I asked.

"They make me happy," she said. And another time: "Didn't you know I always wanted to be an artist?"

I didn't know, didn't remember knowing. We had long since confided all our secrets, I thought, our secret selves. Was this a secret self she had withheld from me?

"Maybe I'll do some sketching too," I said one morning over breakfast, only partly joking.

"I don't want you to," she said with childlike petulance. "Why do you have to share everything I do? Absolutely not."

"I didn't realize they were your gulls," I said. "I had hoped they were in the public domain."

"Don't be an asshole," she said.

In the car, driving to a cocktail party in Edgartown, she reached for my hand. "I'm sorry to be so difficult," she said. "I'm sorry too," I said.

"Sorry that I'm so difficult?" She smiled secretively.

"Sorry that I intruded on your space, sweetheart."

"You're such a nice man," she said.

And though we had apparently made up, a certain tension remained, kept us company like an intruder. We kept making up that summer, enforcing restoration where there had been no apparent breach.

What was going on? I might have asked myself, but the habits of evasion had long-standing claim on me. I got into writing my book, wrote up a case study as if it were a scene in a play, got into my book at the very point where I thought there was no book to write. And I began to play tennis, took a half hour lesson each day, fretted over the flaws in my backhand with a false and displaced seriousness. Adrienne sketched, turned inward. When I talked to her about my book she smiled approvingly, patted me on the head with her smile. She didn't have time to listen to me—the gulls, or something I was unable to imagine, occupied her. It was as if she were pregnant with some new idea about herself, though I didn't know that then.

"Is there something I've done? Are you angry at me?" I remember asking her.

"I haven't thought about it one way or another," she said, offering the same radiant private smile. "I haven't been thinking about you, Yuri."

It was said with a child's directness, without the slightest indication of cruel intent.

"What have you been thinking about?" I asked. Banished from her thoughts, I was in exile from my own good will. I felt punished by her abrupt indifference. My attitude—I see this now— petitioned for forgiveness."

"Whatever it is," she said in the manner of someone with a guilty secret.

I didn't laugh, though her remark struck me funny. "You've been strange this summer," I said. "You know that, don't you?"

"You think I'm strange because I haven't been thinking about you?" she said. "Come on, Yuri."

I overreacted, left the house without explanation, took myself to the edge of the high dune that guarded our private beach. I don't remember exactly how I descended that cliff of sand. There is no direct passage to the beach at that juncture. The next thing I knew I was standing at the water's edge, no other human figure in sight, studying the ferocity of the waves, the ocean in turmoil from some impending storm. My feelings confronted me with the full burden of their outrage. The waves seemed possessed by furies. I walked in in my tennis shorts, gave myself to that presumed manifestation of my feelings, exhilarated by the sense of risk. The second of two extraordinary waves carried me under and held me prisoner until my lungs burned.

I apologized to Adrienne that night after Rebecca had gone to bed, my remarks breaking the extended silence between us.

She had been sitting in bed reading a book called "Birds of New England" when I approached her, and she looked up at me with a benign incongruous smile. "There's nothing to apologize for," she said.

"Just so. I regret storming out of the house the way I did," I said.

"Why was that?" The question asked with wide-eyed sincerity, which I misread as irony. "I wasn't sure why you had left, though I couldn't imagine it had anything to do with me."

I was trying to read her, trying to understand what she was saying or not saying. "You didn't think I was angry at you?"

A flicker of impatience was the only flaw in her maddening calm. She shrugged, went back to her text. I stared at her until she raised her eyes. "I had no idea what was upsetting you, Yuri," she said, "and frankly it didn't interest me."

"It didn't interest you?"

"It was not exactly at the center of my consciousness," she said, seemingly amused at the turn of our conversation. "I'd like to go back to my book if you don't mind."

"I don't know who the fuck I'm talking to," I said. "I think you're a strange visitor from another planet."

She giggled, kept her eyes on the page.

I went away and came back, unable to let go, pulled by the string of her indifference. "Adrienne, I want to know what's going on with you," I said.

She seemed surprised to discover that I still existed, that I was still in the same room. "Yuri, I'm not angry at you," she said with an assurance that was hard to discredit. "I'm just more into myself these days. Don't feel rejected, honey." She smiled like Mother Theresa among the lepers.

"I think you're wrong about what's going on," I said in a conciliatory tone, and took her hand.

She acknowledged my hand only to remove it, to hold

me at arm's length. "Do something by yourself," she said. "Okay? I really want to read. Okay?"

I left her to herself, watched the middle innings of a Red Sox game on television, then went out for a walk in the moonless night. The darkness seemed an appropriate text.

As Adrienne locked hands with herself, I spent more and more time with Rebecca. Or with acquaintances on the island, most of whom were shrinks of one denomination or another. I looked forward to the obligatory cocktail parties, accepted whatever human contact was available, avoided being alone.

Our friends, Peter and Barbara Konig, had a house five miles up island, an inappropriately grandiose A-frame that seemed designed more for pagan worship than as a summer residence. We generally shared dinners with them two or three times a week in the most casual way, never arranging anything more than an hour in advance. Peter was one of my oldest friends and I didn't trouble to distinguish what was habit between us and what was affection. I loved Peter and Barbara, yet I could be exasperated with them, with Peter mostly, but that's another story, only some of which is relevant here.

Peter is a psychoanalyst with a reputation for encouraging the "inner voice" of his therapeutic patients. He tends to encourage the most outrageous acting out and I suspect—this is not an opinion I've kept from him—that he lives off it vicariously. Barbara, who comes from money, who has an income in her own right, is the author of two whimsical children's books, one recently published to respectable reviews. Before she became a writer, she was Peter's secretary, a significant detail in their relationship. We had both been closer to Peter until this summer when Adrienne "discovered" Barbara. "She's more intelligent and articulate," Adrienne reported, "when Peter's not around to intimidate her."

That had not been my experience of Barbara, not at that time.

With the Konigs, Adrienne came out of herself, was notably charming and talkative, a different person from the serene mute that shared my bed and table.

"You've really blossomed this summer," Peter told Adrienne. "I've never seen you look so sensational."

"I don't believe a word of it, Peter," Adrienne said, though I could tell his remark had spoken to her innermost voice. She knew herself to have risen—ascended, I might even say—to a higher stage of development.

And alas I was also charmed by Adrienne's performance around the Konigs, was as much attracted to her that summer as in the passionate early years of our relationship.

The more she withdrew from me, the more, God help me, I felt drawn to her.

When we came home from an evening at the Konigs where she dominated conversation, and laughed giddily at almost anything said, the social butterfly would hide behind the first book or magazine to come to hand. "Did you enjoy yourself?" I might ask, my attempts at conversation becoming increasingly tentative.

"Umm," she might answer.

"You did or you didn't?"

"I told you," she would say. "Why do you keep asking?"

"I want to find out if there's someone else in the room."

It was the same conversation again and again with only cosmetic variation.

"What do you want from me, Yuri?" she would complain. "Why does my separateness bother you?"

"What do I want from you? I want you to treat me as if I don't exist."

Her irritation would flower into a sigh. "That has to be your problem," she would say. "I'm not responsible for you, Yuri. I'm not your mother, baby."

"I get it," I said. "What you're doing is defining by negative example what it is not to be my mother."

"Just fuck off," she said, her voice rising.

When I sat down next to her, she got up from the couch as if I had tilted her from her seat.

She hates me, I said to myself. The news, which seemed all but impossible to believe, left me in a state of panic. Hated by her, I found my own company intolerable.

I had turned forty a month before we left for the Vineyard.

That night, when I finally came to bed, she pretended to be asleep, lying all the way over on her side, facing away, then she came over and put her head on my chest. I kept my arms at my sides.

"What's the matter, honey?" she asked.

"It's nothing," I said in a choked voice.

"Are you crying?"

I didn't answer, fought to gain control of myself, said no.

"There's nothing wrong with crying," she said and returned to her side of the bed, her treatment concluded. "Goodnight."

I lay on my back, staring into the dark, in touch with feelings of rage that were inseparable from grief.

The next few days Adrienne was more like her old self, was kinder and more accessible, though a reserve, a certain wariness, had developed between us. We said good morning at breakfast like acquaintances at a hotel. At lunch, we talked about going to a movie in Vineyard Haven, argued about what to see. Adrienne couldn't make up her mind whether she wanted to go or not, suggested that we ask the Konigs to join us.

I have a clearer recollection of what I wanted to say then what I actually said. What I wanted and didn't want—

ambivalence is always a factor—was to go alone with Adrienne, though I ended up calling Peter and Barbara, who were, as always, happy to join us. There was no necking this time in the back seat of the car. It was our car we took and I was the driver.

We went to the Konigs' place after the movie—I think it was "Tootsie" we saw that night—had ice cream and espresso with them and returned home. Except that we didn't return home. The back right tire of our aging Volvo—the tire farthest from the driver—was completely flat, a fact discovered after driving for a while on a dirt road that seemed to have turned to sand. Adrienne wasn't amused. "You're the one responsible for the car," she said.

It was too dark to change the tire so we left the car at the side of the road and walked back in silence to the Konigs' A-frame, interrupted a shouting match that stopped, it seemed, in midsentence at our unanticipated appearance. Adrienne called the sitter to explain our delay while I had a glass of brandy. When she got off the phone she said, "I forgive you for the tire."

Barbara drove us home, insisted on the prerogative. The two women sat in front, buzzing like flies. Adrienne was giggling at something I hadn't heard. "What's funny?" I asked. "It really can't be explained," Barbara said.

I took the sitter home in the Konigs' silver Mercedes—our live-in girl away that week—while Adrienne and Barbara continued their private talk in our driveway.

Their voices trailed after me and I imagined I heard Adrienne say, "There's something I have to tell you."

When I came into the kitchen on my return, the buzz of conversation died abruptly. Adrienne said in a peremptory voice, showing off, "Be a dear and open a bottle of white wine, Yuri."

I uncorked the bottle and poured three glasses of wine. "Anything else I can do to make myself of use?" I asked.

Barbara laughed, Adrienne studied the tile floor. "You're a shit," she whispered.

Later, when Barbara had gone home, I asked Adrienne what they had been talking about on my arrival. "Nothing that concerns you," Adrienne said.

I let it go, couldn't let it go. "You stopped talking as soon as you were aware of me," I said.

She gave me an amused mocking look, a sassy child's look. "What would you say to a patient if he said something like that to you?"

"As you well know," I said, "not all suspicion is evidence of paranoia. I want to know what it is I'm not supposed to hear."

"If you're not supposed to hear it, you don't get to hear it," she said in her dreamy voice. She offered a mock-shudder, put her arm on my shoulder. "Oh Yuri, why would we be talking about you. We were being silly, baby." She bumped me playfully with her hip. "Do you want to explore the problem?" she said in her therapist's voice.

If her signals were mixed, I responded only to the positive ones. I took her to bed. We took each other to bed, I suppose. It surprised me how hungry I was for her, how much hunger had been stored up.

"That was nice," she said afterward. She put her head on my chest, her hair which was in a loose bun tangled in my beard, and I fell asleep that way. Her head bruised my heart with its weight.

The next day when I went to the Konigs to retrieve my car, I got into an extended conversation with Peter who was having his own domestic difficulties. Barbara, in what Peter referred to as a palace revolution, was demanding a salary for typing up his case notes, something she used to do as a matter of course. Peter didn't mind paying a salary, he said—her rates were quite reasonable—but objected to the implications of the demand. "I resent being made into a sexist villain," he said. "My feminist patients have a very different view of me."

I drove to the Shell Station in Menemsha where I dropped off the tire for repair, Peter coming along for the ride. "Barbara mentioned that you were having some problems at home," he said at some point. "I'm sorry as hell, buddy."

I offered no news, was irritated at the pleasure he seemed to take in his own solicitousness. So Adrienne had lied to me, had used Barbara and Peter to deliver a message she had been unwilling to give me directly. I muttered something about there being palace revolutions everywhere.

"This is post-civilization, buddy," he said, an old line of his. "Divorce has become an obligation to the self. I feel for both of you. I want you to know that. I love you both."

Such claims of affection demanded the response of gratitude, which I offered almost willingly.

I stayed for lunch at the Konigs, in no hurry to confront Adrienne about her lie. Barbara and Peter played out the contentions of their marriage over a cold linguini dish with pesto, olives and artichoke hearts. I was there to witness their performance, to validate its necessity, though I left before the final curtain.

I took Rebecca to the ocean beach in the afternoon and later to the tennis club for a lesson while Adrienne did whatever it was she did.

"Did you have a good day?" she asked at the close of an almost silent dinner.

"Okay," I said. "Bad in the morning, good in the afternoon."

"I had a wonderful day," she said, "being completely alone."

"Why not?" I said. Rebecca came over and sprawled on my lap.

"You really don't know what it's like," she said. "You need to have people around you, Yuri, or you feel empty."

"I don't recall telling you that," I said.

"Guys," Rebecca said, "this is not an argument we're having."

"No argument," said Adrienne. "I'm just making an observation about Yuri."

"Let me understand this," I said, tasting my bitterness as if it were food the system had refused to digest. "You observe the emptiness I feel inside when I'm alone. You must be endowed with x-ray vision." A cheap remark, unworthy of us.

"I find this discussion extremely tiresome," my disaffected wife said and got up from the table. "Please excuse me."

The next day, or the next, Adrienne sought me out to apologize for what she described as her need to live within herself more. She could understand, she said, that it was causing me some unhappiness, though it was not her intention to hurt me. "I've been changing and I don't think you've noticed—you can be so oblivious, Yuri—or maybe you haven't been willing to accept the change in me."

I refused the bait this time, struggled to appear reasonable. "If you want us to live differently. Adrienne, tell me what you have in mind."

"I don't know," she said. "I'm not even sure that the way I want to live includes you."

Even given the estrangement of recent weeks, the remark shocked me, provoked panic.

"I don't know what to make of what you tell me," I said, or imagined myself saying. I thought of asserting that I continued to love her as if the burden of her apparent rejection of me were a demand for reassurance. "Is there someone else?" I let myself ask.

"There's only me," she said with just enough hesitation to suggest the possibility of another answer.

I willed self-control at the price of denying the pain I felt. "You're disappointed with your life, want something else, is that it?"

She gave me a sly grin, offered the room a sigh. "It's not even that I'm discontent, as you put it, Yuri. In some ways, I'm more at peace with myself than I've ever been. Can you understand that? It's just that I feel there's something missing in my life. I feel that we haven't risked enough."

It was like a dream in which everyone around you is speaking an indecipherable foreign language. "What haven't we risked?" I asked. "Are you talking about fucking other people?"

It looked for a moment as if she might give an answer, her eyes turned inward studying private scripture. "Interview is over," she said briskly. "I'd like to read now if it's all right with you." She picked up a copy of "Psychology Today" and covered her face with it.

When I turned away, she said from behind her mask, "You have to learn to be less dependent on me."

It was as if a switch had been pushed that summer and the process of our disaffection set irreversibly in motion. It was tacky stuff, unworthy, though deeply compelling. We did what we could, Adrienne and I, moved tacitly into what had the appearance of a formal agreement. Our marriage became its own shadow. We stayed away from one another in private, though we gave the impression in public some of the time at least of being the devoted couple outsiders imagined us to be. The last thing to come apart were appearances. I am getting ahead of myself.

Peter dropped over one afternoon when Adrienne and Rebecca were out picking strawberries or taking a swim to tell me that Ted and Diane Fieldstone had split up after thirteen years. The news offered no great surprise. The previous fall Diane had published a satiric novel about psychoanalysts in which a man like her husband had been portrayed as a tedious hypocrite. The book seemed a not easily forgivable betrayal, though Ted seemed to take the novel in stride, allowed himself to manifest pleasure in his wife's success.

Eight months after the book's publication, Ted had left Diane, had flown off the Vineyard to spend a few days with friends in Boston.

"I told Ted on the phone," Peter reported, "that he had put all our marriages in jeopardy by running off."

"Peter, if inconsistency were a virtue," I said, "you'd be a candidate for sainthood. Had Barbara written a book like Diane's, you would have walked out on her before the jacket cover had been designed."

"Absolutely not," he said. "I might have kicked the shit out of Barbara if she attacked me in print, but I would never have broken up our marriage over it."

"You see wife beating, then, as the more moral of the two alternatives?"

"That's middle-class bullshit, buddy, and you know it. A man throws a punch at his wife is making a statement about his feelings for her. Barbara knows that."

We got into one of our theoretical arguments, though it was more heated, more acrimonious than usual. "You're a fraud," I shouted at him. "You only believe the things you say the moment you hear yourself say them."

"You're a bigger fraud, buddy," he shouted back. "I'll tell you what I can't believe, what I can't believe is that you've never taken a poke at the provocative lady you share your bed with."

I said something about his living vicariously through other people's aggressions, then seeing the look on his face— Peter is more vulnerable than he lets on—I realized that I had gone too far. I made a joke about our long standing competitiveness.

He passed me to retrieve his beer and we inadvertently bumped shoulders. "You were in the way," he said.

"I wasn't moving," I said.

"It so happens I had right of way," he said. "The rule is, offensive player has right of way on the defensive man's court."

"I think it's called hospitality," I said. I held out my hand and Peter took it, embracing me with his other arm.

"Yuri, last Christmas, Barbara bought me a pair of boxing gloves. I'm embarrassed to tell you this, though why should I be. Sometimes we spar before going to bed. It converts hostility into sexual energy. I'm thinking of doing a paper on it."

"In my house we tend to spar with words," I said.

"That's a mistake," he said. "Words hurt feelings. Words create real wounds."

Adrienne and Rebecca came in. Rebecca embraced me and Adrienne gave Peter an enthusiastic kiss. "The ocean is wonderful today," she said. "It's as gentle and sweet-natured as a lover."

"That sounds like an attractive recommendation," Peter said. Adrienne giggled as if Peter's remark contained more wit than I had noticed.

Peter's departure was occasion for Adrienne's withdrawal. She took her sketchpad out on the deck, asked in passing if I would entertain Rebecca while she worked.

I followed my disaffected wife on to the deck and stood over her until she acknowledged my presence. I was in a fever, a blind stupefied rage. Rebecca stood behind me, tugging on my shirt. It was fortunate for that. Our child saved us, gave us a temporary reprieve. I know I would have regretted what I was about to do, though it seemed at the moment the only appropriate response. There is worse to come.

Four

The Search for Identity

I haven't written in this journal for two weeks now. Reasons will make their appearance. It's the abruptness of what happened that surprises me. And yet I see it in retrospect as something that was bound to happen. I see it as something I had denied myself for too long. The details move backwards like a film shown in reverse.

I have always had faith in the fortuitous. In some superstitious pocket, I believe that my life has already been played out. I come to it after the fact, collecting clues as I go.

The man happened to be coming down the street in my direction just as I finished my session at the hospital. A coincidence I immediately distrusted. I was outraged at his presumption. I demanded to know what he was doing on my street. He had a work space in the neighborhood, he said, he was an art student, smiling in a way that made me disbelieve him all the more. I told him that I thought he was lying. He challenged me to come with him and see his studio with my own eyes. So I went along with him to catch him in his lie. (I had nothing else in mind.) There were four flights of stairs (two double flights) to climb. First impressions: the studio he showed me (I still didn't believe it was his) was like an elaborate stage set. It had a brass double bed on a platform set off by a winding staircase. There were three or four paintings on the wall which were dark and technically crude.

Also unexpectedly delicate. The sensibility of the paintings was surprisingly delicate. (So I was taken by surprise. There was more to him than I had been willing to see.) One of the paintings, a portrait of two women (with the same face), seemed almost good. In his space, as he called it, he was gentlemanly, even deferential. We had vinegary white wine in matching coffee mugs. We exchanged commonplaces. Then I said (or someone impersonating me said), "Now that you've got me here, we might as well get on with it." He professed to be shocked, an inspired touch. "I admire you too much, Adrienne," he said. (He pronounced my name correctly.)

I laughed at him. I called him a reluctant seducer. I was absolutely sure of what I wanted. (I was not myself. I did not feel like myself.) "You told me you envied my husband," I said. "Was that just a tease?"

He refused to take me at my word. The more shy he played, the more insistent I became. "You know how to seduce," I said, "but you don't know how to give in."

"You're giving me a headache," he said. "What about your husband? What is he going to think about this?"

"I'm interested in a sexual encounter," this person I was impersonating said. "I'm not interested in discussing my life with you. I have a good marriage. I love my husband."

"I want you to be absolutely sure that this is what you want," he said. (I nodded, whispered yes.) "Okay. It's your funeral." (Hearing himself, he laughed.) "I didn't mean that the way it sounded."

As we climbed the winding stairs to his balcony (it was like an altar in the sky), I began to panic. (You're being bad, I told myself. It's about time, I answered. I repeated the phrase to myself in the middle of things. "It's about time.")

There are worse betrayals than sleeping with someone other than your husband. The worst betrayals are betrayals of self.

I have a patient whose husband has left her after a marriage of thirty-one years. Her courage shames me. She is terribly (painfully) lonely. Her children are all grown, have separate lives. It is an act of will for her to get through the day. The vestiges of a lifelong dependence continue to hobble her. A life without taking care of someone seems unimaginable. She tends to mother her lovers and frighten them away. She has been dependent on the dependence of her husband and children for so long. I tell her nothing that she doesn't already know. (I help her to clarify.) I tell her what she knows and she has not be able to fully accept: that she has not loved her husband for the longest time. I feed off her anger as she feeds off my support. At times, I feel myself taking on her sadness. I am furious at her husband for leaving her (and me, I feel) for a woman twenty years younger. I want to shake the man. I want to tell him, "You are not worthy of this woman you left." What we share is a father's defection—hers died when she was twelve, mine moved out when I was eight. We both know that the men we love betray us eventually. That knowledge is engraved in us.

Yuri asks me (in bed of all places) if I'm still seeing Carroway.

"Not as a regular patient," I say. Even in evasion, I feel it necessary to tell a version of the truth.

"Do you mind," he asks, "if I see Mrs. Carroway as a patient?"

"Why should I mind?" I say.

"If you were still seeing Carroway, it might create complications."

"I told you I wasn't, didn't I?" My voice is shrill. "What do you want from me, Yuri?" Panic gathers. My smile is like a mask.

"Have I missed something?" He does a double take, a routine that used to amuse me. "Are you pissed off at me because I was right about Carroway?"

"You're so wrong, Yuri. You couldn't be more wrong."

"The man has a reputation as a seducer of shop girls," he says. "He's a classic sociopath."

The phrase "seducer of shop girls" makes me giggle. "Oh Yuri," I say and touch his arm. "You don't have to put Carroway down. You're not in competition with him." I put my arms around him. Yuri. Yuri.

"I'd rather you didn't take on Mrs. Carroway," I say.

I think of what I've done as characteristic yet unlike me. It happened that once and I am clear that it will not happen again. If Carroway makes any attempt to renew contact, I will tell him (I talk to myself the words) that I have no interest in seeing him again. I am even thinking of not going to the hospital on Thursday (I can call in sick) to avoid a confrontation. It has always been hard for me to refuse a direct request. The "good girl" wants to say yes to whatever is asked. She needs to please. Yuri has been particularly sweet these last few days. He senses my pulling away. (It's as if he knows but doesn't know he knows.)

My father, when he was young (my father was always young), was a charming and charismatic man. He was the most charming man. It was not his fault (nor mine) that my mother didn't want a husband. When she married Spencer, she got a man who would never trouble her. My father's dead now. My stepfather has never been fully alive.

I delayed leaving the hospital. I got drawn into a conversation with my supervisor (a jealous, mean-spirited lady), from which it was difficult to break free. It was a relief not to find Carroway waiting for me on the steps. The man is sensitive to my feelings, I let myself think. He is aware that

I don't want our thing (our thing that is really no-thing) to continue. It strikes me as I record my feelings that I am not telling myself everything I know. I feel grateful to Carroway for his tact and walking to the subway, I consider stopping by his loft to thank him. I feel no danger in making this unannounced visit. I am completely and perfectly calm. A black teenager makes an obscene remark as our paths cross. This ruffles me only a little. I let myself take it as appreciation. I feel radiant. I feel absolutely elegant. It is a blissful day to walk and I decide to go to the subway by way of Carroway's loft, a slightly longer route. I will acknowledge the gracefulness of his behavior. I will thank him and leave.

I go through several changes of mood going up the four flights of stairs. I consider retracing my steps as I approach the door. I must take responsibility, I tell myself. I have made a decision, I have come this far. There is nothing to do but knock at the door and complete my errand. I am a great distance from my feelings. I am in a state of weatherless calm.

There is no answer to my knock. I listen (suspiciously) for sounds of movement inside. Thursday is his afternoon at his space, he told me. I tend to believe what I'm told. I knock again. If intent were enough, I would knock down the door. I've been a presumptuous lady. Yes? (I can feel myself unravelling.) My seducer of shop girls has made a point of avoiding his shopworn therapist. (How else explain his absence?) I would sit down on the steps but they are filthy and there is nothing to put under my skirt. I give myself fifteen minutes, then a five minute extension on the fifteen. Then (I have waited so long already) another five minutes. (I am not, am I, this fallen woman, waiting to see her seducer?) I return down the stairs. I am feeling fragile, slightly damaged. On the second landing, I hear someone coming. "I'm glad I didn't miss you," he says, taking my hand. "I had an appointment with my lawyer. You know how it is." There is no occasion to thank him for his tact. I forget why I'm there.

"I really have to get home," I say, going back up the stairs with him.

I have come this far. And he is so overjoyed, so persuasively overjoyed, to have me here. "I know I don't want to go on with this," I say, though I follow him up the devious steps to his balcony. It no longer seems like an altar to me. More like a stage this time. A place for performance. He congratulates me when it is over. "You were sensational," he says. I feel myself blushing. I am pleased and touched. (I am the secretive girl my stepfather disapproved of.) I am on a high. (I feel I can do anything I want.) It is a scary scary feeling.

When I come in, Yuri looks at me as if he knows everything. His eyes are narrowed. (I know that look.) "What happened?" he asks.

"What do you mean what happened?" So much for belligerence. Then I make my excuse. "The train broke down," I say. "We didn't move for almost an hour."

"I know how awful that can be," he says. "I always panic in trains when they don't move. Why don't I fix you a gin and tonic."

His solicitude offends me. "What I really need is a hot shower, Yuri. And would it be so terrible if I had some private time after doing clinic?"

"The way you put it," he says, "implies that I'm the one who's keeping you from doing what you want. Is that realistic?" "Don't fight," Rebecca says. "We'll agree that it's not realistic." How blind he is, I think. "Can we talk about it after I take my shower?" I say. It is not a question, though I wait for his reply, frozen in place.

Rebecca embraces me from behind, startles me. "What are you doing?" I scream at her. I feel that everyone has turned against me. Why won't you let me be loveable to you? (Don't love me so much.)

If I don't pull myself away, I will stay at the bottom of

these stairs forever. I go up. I lock myself in the bathroom. I undress for the second time.

I think of myself as a bad person who has been wronged by being thought of as a bad person.

I do (did) what I have to do. I discover who I am by doing what is necessary to be myself.

In the shower, I feel charged with energy. And I think: what is it? What is it that I am feeling? I can barely breathe I am so terribly alive. (What is really going on?) I am a child in the shower. I sing. I abandon myself. (I feel myself abandoned.) And Yuri lets me go on with it. Yuri doesn't care. Yuri no longer cares for me.

Five

Transference

_____

Let me set the scene. I am packing the car in a desultory way when Peter and Barbara drive up to say goodbye. We are leaving the Vineyard three days early because the weather— it is our mutually agreed on excuse—has failed us. We have been shrouded in mist, our view of the ocean denied us for almost a week. Barbara scurries in the house to see Adrienne after giving me the kind of kiss mourners exchange at funerals. My memory to this point is absolute.

Peter sidles up as is his style, his posture itself an unacceptable insinuation. "Depression is not the way to nirvana, buddy," he says. He puts his arm on my shoulder and I shrug it off. "I'm feeling for you, you asshole," he says.

There's more of the same—Peter's infuriating conde-scension, my benumbed packing of the car—before all hell breaks loose, but I want to cut away to something that happened the morning of the day before. The scene moves indoors.

"You and mommy are very weird with each other this summer," Rebecca was saying. We were sitting on a rug in front of the fireplace playing Monopoly while Adrienne, at the other end of the long room, sketched imaginary birds. I thought for a while— she seemed to be studying us—that we were her subject.

I made some lame remark about people who are together a lot of the time needing periods of separateness.

"Is that anything like a divorce?" said my precocious daughter. She knew about divorces from the broken homes of several of her classmates at Brearley.

I defended the status quo. "Your mother and I have no plans to get a divorce," I said.

"Is that a promise, daddy—you'll never get divorced?"

"No one can say for certain what's going to happen in the future," I said.

"That's what you always say," said my world-weary opponent.

"You're confusing me with your other parents," I said.

Adrienne laughed. Rebecca reminded me that I had landed on Chance and was required to pick a card. The arrival of one of Rebecca's friends interrupted the game. The card I picked was "Get Out of Jail Free."

"You handled that well," Adrienne said to me later when Rebecca was outside playing with her friend Tanya.

"What would you have said?" I asked her, but she was already out of the room, had moved on to the porch. I repeated my question and when she ignored it a second time, I came up from behind and put my arms around her. She put her hands over mine. We stood there like that for something like fifteen seconds, then she said, "Yuri, you always make gestures that are willed rather than felt. You know that's true, baby." She removed my arms like untying a package.

Her assertion provoked denial. And yet she was right, right enough to make me question my motives. Consciousness, I wanted to say, did not preclude feeling, but she knew all that. Our way of seeing things was so much the same, our insights so interconnected, that our conversation remained implicit, required no voice. Our roles had been defined by unspoken agreement. I was the prisoner of consciousness, she was the sprite of feeling, a medium for unexamined and uncontrolled urges.

I am aware that the scene I am describing has not been brought to conclusion, remains on the page, as it does in my feelings, permanently incomplete. We seemed to play the same inconclusive scene again and again that summer (that fall, that winter) in intricate variation.

The next thing I remember—clearly some steps have been repressed—Peter and I were rolling around on the damp grass, punching one another.

Barbara was screaming something at us that sounded like "don't you dare" and sometimes my name and sometimes his. I broke his nose while he was on the ground, broke it with my elbow or with my forearm, heard the crack or felt it when I hammered the side of his head with my arm. Barbara was pulling my hair and I remember getting up and holding out my hand to Peter. "I'm sorry, buddy," I think I said. Barbara helped Peter into the car—he was bent over, his eyes tearing, nose out of joint—and they drove away. Adrienne and Rebecca shunned me when I came in, were in Rebecca's room with the door closed.

I floated through the silent house like an unwelcomed hero, high on acting out, resenting the betrayal of those closest. Peter, who was an advocate of hands-on expression of feelings, had been treated with his own medicine. My knuckles ached with pleasure. It was instinctive what I had done, uncharacteristic and unexpected, therefore valuable. I was riding the displacement express, exhilaration receding as reality gradually returned. I finished packing the car in virtual slow motion. "Why did you do such a thing," Rebecca asked me when I saw her again.

"He did something I didn't like," I said.

"You don't like me to fight when someone does something I don't like," she said.

"Sometimes," I said, "we do things we don't approve of for our children."

"It's not Peter you were angry at," Adrienne said. And

65

then a moment later when Rebecca was out of the room. "I hope you know that was a cowardly thing to do."

I took her reprimand to heart, which is to say I drove back to the city under a cloud of depression and self-loathing.

Rebecca forgave me the disappointment my behavior had caused her as soon as we reached home. "You must have had good reasons, daddy," she said, hugging me an extra long time when I put her to bed. "Please don't let it happen again." She laughed at herself, at her parody of me.

"I'll try to do better," I promised.

"I'm glad it was his nose and not yours," she said.

The first time that Peter and I ran into each other at clinic, he put his arm on my shoulder. "I missed you, buddy," he said. Though pleased to be forgiven, I found myself, unaccountably, unforgiving.

"When I called," I said, "Barbara said you weren't talking to me." His nose was still swollen.

"That's Barbara's thing," he said. "For my part, Yuri, I wish you only well. I hope things are going better for you on the home court. So?"

"Things are better at home," I said, full of sufferer's pride. "It's good we're still friends," I mumbled, moving on.

The next time our paths crossed at the hospital, we avoided looking at each other.

Adrienne called Barbara at some point in the hopes of repairing that half of the friendship.

I found her in the bedroom when I came home from clinic, lying in fetal position with a pillow covering her face. "Is that you, Yuri?" she asked from thousands of miles away. "I'm feeling bombed out, honey. Would you look after dinner?" I sat down on the edge of the bed and took her hand. Her eyes were puffed and red. "What happened?"

"Go away, Yuri. Please. I mean it."

"Tell me what happened."

"If you don't go away, I'll scream," she said in a whisper. She looked like a child.

"I don't mind if you scream," I said.

She mouthed a scream, a mock scream, a real scream mocked. "I promise I'll tell you later, Yuri," she said. "Okay? I need to be alone at this time, baby. I really do. Barbara gave me a horrendous time."

I reproduce this conversation—half real, half imagined— because I knew, as I walked away, that I was once more failing her test.

That wasn't all. The next day, coming upstairs from the office, I overheard Adrienne talking on the phone, heard her saying that she didn't know she could ever forgive Barbara. When I came into the bedroom she made a show of lowering her voice. When I looked at her she waved me away and though I couldn't understand why she needed to exclude me—at first I waved back, mocking her gesture—I returned downstairs, accepted my dismissal.

As soon as I was out of the room her voice rose again so that it seemed that she meant me to hear her side of the conversation, that she was using the call as a form of communication between us. "Look Barbara, I said," I heard her say, "Yuri and I are not the same person. I'm not responsible for his bad behavior."

When she got off the phone, I asked her who she was talking to. "That's my business," she said. "Why do you involve yourself in my business?"

"We happen to be married," I said.

"I want you to respect my privacy," she said in the voice of empty threat. "I don't want to be questioned about what I do or who I talk to. Do you understand?"

"I understand," I said. "I just want to know who you were talking to on the phone."

"My life is my own," she said, "and if you can't get used to that, maybe you ought to take off. I don't need you here."

"You go too far," I said. We stood glaring at each other, maybe a foot apart, neither willing to yield ground.

Our separate rages played off one another like images in a mirror.

"Your problem, Yuri, is that you don't go far enough," she said as if she were disappointed to discover this failing in me. Needing to prove her wrong, I walked out of the house without explanation, banged the door melodramatically behind me.

Does it matter what happened? Or that nothing happened. I spent the next couple of hours talking distractedly to a woman in a bar, small, dark, of no particular age. She seemed amused, even turned on, by my distraction. We talked about talking and listening, as a matter of fact. I confided that I liked to talk so much that listening to others required enormous constraint for me. It was a truth about myself I had not recognized before.

I walked her home a little after midnight and we kissed at the door of her place. Then we went inside together. She said if we went to bed, she would want me to stay the night. Those were her terms. I said I couldn't manage that. We pressed against each other, she brushed her hand through my hair. I took her number and left.

When I came home, Adrienne was upstairs—most of the house lights out—and I watched the last third of a movie on TV before going up to bed. In the movie a man has left his wife for a younger woman and at the end he is left in turn by the woman for a younger man.

I slipped under the covers—Adrienne was sleeping in the center of the bed—conscious of heaviness, feeling swollen and out of shape, conscious of not wanting Adrienne to wake. I was imagining how my time with the woman in the bar would have seemed in a movie. Would the man have seemed more sympathetic to an audience if he stayed with the woman or if he left? A moment or so after I closed my eyes, Adrienne whispered something that sounded like, "Are you crying, Yuri?"

I said nothing, reached for her, put my hand on her shoulder. She put her hand over mine, then removed it as if her fingers had been burned. "Why won't you let me sleep?" she said. "Go fuck yourself," I said in a hoarse voice.

"If you don't let me sleep," she said after a moment, hesitantly, "I'll sleep somewhere else. Is that what you want?"

I turned on my side away from her, laughed at something, felt crazed.

She rested her hand on my back. "Do you want me to leave, Yuri?"

"I don't care," I lied.

She huddled on her side. "I'm going to sleep," she announced as if there were more than one other person listening to her.

Why am I reporting this mundane conversation? Because, I answer myself, meanings reside in mundane details. I am trying to understand what was going on between us— the dynamic of our deteriorating relationship—so I return again and again to the same or similar scenes, looking for clues.

I return to this sleepless night, which goes on and on, a waking dream of hell. I doze and come alive, sleep for minutes at a time, turn from back to side like a metronome. Adrienne sleeps or seems to sleep.

I get up, go downstairs, have a brandy, come back to bed.

"Make up your mind," Adrienne says as if she had been rehearsing the remark to herself for hours.

"What about?" I ask after a prolonged silence. "What are you talking about?"

She matches my silence and takes it a beat further. "Whether you want to sleep in this bed or walk around," she says.

"I wouldn't mind getting it on," I whisper.

She laughs, which is unexpected, bumps my leg with hers. "I don't know. I don't know."

I roll over on top of her and she reluctantly (perhaps not), puts her arms around me. I put my mouth on her breast, the cotton of her nightgown between us. Her breathing quickens.

At some point, we both seem to turn to stone as if bewitched.

We stay this way for prolonged minutes, an embrace of statues, frozen in time. In my memory of it, we never come apart.

I was aware in that embrace, memory reports, of hating her, which was a new feeling for me or new in its intensity. I had no tenderness for her, or too much to acknowledge. Anger was the only thing in me that wanted to make love. My feelings horrified me and I rolled off her corpse, moved in defeat to my side of the bed. Sleep, which had rejected me, took me in hand.

"Are you all right, honey?" Adrienne asked from across the void.

I didn't say anything because I was asleep, or moving into sleep, her question too far away to acknowledge. Of course, I'm all right, I imagined myself saying, heard myself say in the privacy of dream. Why wouldn't I be all right? Her answer to my silence echoed, revised itself over and over and never was right, never gave satisfaction.

I had a succession of nightmares that night. Sleep's hands were rough.

Six

The Language of the Self

I am this bad person, I have always been made to believe. It is my stepfather's idea of me. It is Yuri's idea. I am my mother's bad self. (I've been a prisoner of other people's definitions.) It is not even my reflection in the mirror, but Yuri's version (I was going to write virgin) of me. The bad Adrienne. For more than twelve years, I've been living as Yuri's shadow. That's not quite right either. I tend not to be inarticulate so much as bereft of language. Unparented by language. Language's orphan. As I was my mother's idea of a daughter (though she never approved, never really loved me for it), I became Yuri's idea of a wife. I was not Yuri's shadow, but his female image of himself in fantasy's mirror. I was the not-Yuri part of Yuri. I existed for him as if he had imagined me in a novel or a movie: the smart, sexy, happy wife who was (in his image) also a shrink. Except I wasn't always deliriously happy with the arrangement. I knew of course that it was my failure, this deficiency, that I was still the same bad girl my father fled (and my step-father beat), and who wouldn't (couldn't) please my saintly mother and that there was some hidden, nasty part of me (I was always a secret terrorist in my heart) that couldn't leave well enough alone.

There were rewards. There are rewards for being good. If I took care of Yuri, if I took care to hide my bad self, he would have to love me. I was ready to do almost anything (wash windows, take out the garbage, anything) to be loved. At the same time, the bad child (my hidden self) knew it was a lie. Who could love me? I was an article of use. I was other people's fantasy of wife, daughter, mother, lover, window washer, therapist, whatever. And I wasn't in this alone. Yuri has to bear some of the blame. (One morning love, wearing only a scarf, walked out the door never to return.) Yuri didn't notice what was happening. If he loved me enough, he would never have allowed things to go so far. I suspect he was collecting grievances. (We all do some of that, don't we?) I couldn't like that about him.

These are my reasons. I thought—How could I continue to see Carroway if I loved Yuri? I thought—If I was really happy with Yuri, I wouldn't have needed Carroway. And so on. Because I found myself in love with someone not my husband (I was no longer the good person who was Yuri's wife), I stopped loving Yuri. It had to happen. We had been like two organisms breathing out of the same lung. The air began to get too thin. I had to tear myself free in order to breathe.

As I got free of Yuri (or mostly free), he began to seem less real. It was as if he was fading (like an old photograph) before my eyes. He was there (moving around the house, eating dinner with us, sharing my bed), but not really there. He had become his own ghost to me. The shade of Yuri. I was sad that he had died, though it bothered me that, though dead, he continued to assert his needs. Look how I'm suffering, his shadowy presence announced. You must help me, this ghost insisted, you must take care of me. Even if I wanted to help him (if only to like myself better), what could I do for him? He was no longer real. I tried to be kind, but it made him angrier. (His grievance occupied the house like an overstayed guest.) There was nothing I could do.

Our friend Peter says that I take pleasure in being the bad person in the movie of our lives. Maybe so. The bad person's secret is that she is really better (more audacious, more interesting, more alive) than the so-called good person. She makes it possible for the good person to take satisfaction in his goodness.

I've been seeing Carroway for almost a year, not counting the August Yuri, Rebecca and I spent on the Vineyard. I've been seeing him for a year but rarely more than once a week. (Thursday is our day.) So I am taken aback when he calls to ask me to meet him at his studio this (Saturday) afternoon. It requires making last minute arrangements for Rebecca and lying to Yuri, neither of which I like to do. Still, it is a habit I have difficulty denying myself. If I can get a sitter, I tell Carroway, I'll be there at two o'clock.

Arrangements fall into place with ominous ease. Yuri, who has had a patient cancel, agrees to take Rebecca to The Museum of Natural History. Have a good time, he calls to me as I go out the door. Someone taps at the window. I turn and wave to the house, stumble, nearly fall over backwards. (All my loved ones, I think.)

I am a few minutes early, arrive before Carroway. Let myself in with my key. The loft seems smaller now that I am used to it, less imposing.

Without taking off my coat, I look at the painting on Carroway's easel (it's one Carroway's been unable to solve) and I see with absolute clarity where it fails. It asks to be made right. At first, holding the brush an inch or so from the canvas, I pantomime revising it.

The right hand is badly drawn. I paint on his picture, improve it just enough to show him how it might be made better.

When I hear someone on the steps, I put down the

brush (clean it), make myself at home on my side of the loft. (I will tell him before he discovers what I've done.)

Carroway, wearing dark glasses, comes in in long nervous strides. He goes up to the painting without acknowledging my presence. "Hey, it's beginning to look like something," he says without irony.

I come over to him, still not out of my coat. I kiss him on the side of the mouth. "I know what it needs," I say.

"It needs what we all need. It needs some loving," he says, moving away from me. He takes off his leather jacket and hangs it carefully on the brass coat tree. I put my coat on the branch below.

"You look like you haven't been sleeping," I say.

"Anna Marie's been on my case," he says "I got like two hours of shuteye last night, if that."

I hold out my hand to him. "Tell me about it, baby," I say.

"You look sensational, babe," he says, still glancing at his unfinished painting. "I don't want to talk about it this minute, okay? Would you make us some coffee?" He won't look at me.

I know what's coming and I'm not prepared to handle it.

"I almost wrote you a letter," he says. "You know the paint looks like it's still wet. I think the fucking super comes in and fucking works on my paintings when I'm not around."

"You're not around right now," I say.

"Yeah," he says. "I feel wired. You're a super-smart lady, Adrienne. Classy and super-perceptive. It really knocked me out that someone like you was interested in me. Look, babe, why don't we sit down on the red couch. Okay?"

"I prefer to stand," I say.

We are sitting on the red leather couch when he tells me that he has promised Anna Marie not to see me again. They, Carroway and Anna Marie (and God knows who else), are going to evaluate what they have together. They need to find out if their marriage can be saved.

I offer no reaction. "I wish you luck," I say.

"That's a classy thing to say," he says with worked up sincerity. He squeezes my arm. "It's dangerous, Adrienne, for me to sit too close to you, you know?"

There's more. He offers me the compensation of saving my own marriage which he knows (he says) to be important to me. (It's over, I say to myself. And still it seems wrong.) Who does he think he's talking to?

I am at the coat tree, though I don't remember getting up from the couch. When I try to put on my coat the arm holes seem to have disappeared. "I'm going," I announce, though the floor holds me in place.

"I felt very sexy when I came here," I say.

"You looked terrifically sexy," he says, noticing me for the first time. (I believe him even though I know he lies.) I hurry to the door, my coat over my arm. My hand on the door knob (which won't turn), I remember something I forgot to tell him. "You'll never have with Anna Marie what you had with me," I say.

When Carroway opens the door for me, I spike him with an elbow (my worst moment). And hurry away. Panic chases me down the stairs.

Yuri and Rebecca are playing a board came called Othello at the kitchen table when I come in. I mumble something and go upstairs.

I am lying in bed with the covers over my face. I hear the door open. I imagine Yuri is looking into the bedroom, staring at me. (Why doesn't he say something?)

Rebecca clears her throat to get my attention. "Is that you, Bec?" I hear myself say. "Mommy's not feeling well. Come over and give me a hug."

Rebecca takes a long time to approach. She lifts the

covers, kisses the top of my head. We both laugh. I put my arms around her. say "Mommy loves you."

"Are you going to sleep?" she asks. "Daddy wants to know what your plans are."

"Does he?" I say. "You tell him if he wants to know, he can ask me himself."

I close my eyes to shut out the light. When I open them I see Yuri standing in the doorway. He does not look friendly. "Rebecca said you wanted to see me," he says.

I prop myself up to look at him. (He seems less shadowy, more in focus.) "How are you, Yuri?" I say, my voice miles away. "I've hardly noticed you in the past couple months. How have you been holding up, baby?"

He sits down at the foot of the bed. (It is odd how touched I am by him.) "You can come closer," I tell him.

"I know you're involved with someone," he says, his voice pitiless. "I want to know who it is."

I press my face to the pillow. "What?"

"I want to know what's going on?" he says.

"Doesn't it matter to you that I'm very upset," I say into the pillow. "Please, honey. I'll talk to you tonight after Rebecca goes to bed."

"You've put me through hell," he mutters. (I think it is what he says.) He goes out the door and closes it with a bang. (My head splits.) He betrays me by missing the point. He is having an affair with his suffering.

Seven

Counter-Transference

As my marriage deteriorated, I became increasingly distracted with my patients. Drifting off into fantasy, confusing details and names, falling into private obsession. I found myself identifying with the mistreated lovers of certain women patients, with one in particular.

There was an inappropriate harshness in my voice as I pointed out to Melinda Goldhart that her behavior toward the boyfriend she complained endlessly about was provocative and self-fulfilling. "Don't you see," I threw at her like stones, "the man behaves badly because you want him to behave badly."

She shook loose a tear. I was supposed to feel sorry for mistreating her. Instead, I felt annoyance, wanted to shake some real tears out of that calculating soul. I was also aware—dimly—that these feelings were inappropriate, that I was behaving unprofessionally, that I was out of control.

Why do I go on like this?

This is not a confession but an investigation into feeling. I am imperfect.

Melinda's parents had refused all authority, had pretended to Melinda that she could do anything she liked. They had offered her a world without boundaries, a dazzling chaos. Every step was a step off a precipice into space. The simplest acts for Melinda engendered paralyzing anxieties.

When Melinda first went into treatment with me she rarely talked during the therapy session. She withheld speech willfully, talked to me in her head, as she later reported, but could barely articulate a complex sentence in my presence. She was afraid of exposing her secrets, she said. We tried different arrangements to make her feel less vulnerable. For a while, we sat with the backs of our chairs together. She worried when she couldn't see me that I had gone away, or was reading a book, or had gone to sleep.

"What are you doing now?" she would ask from time to time.

"Why don't you turn around and see for yourself," I said.

She sometimes turned, sometimes didn't.

The same or almost the same conversation repeated like an echo. The repetition seemed to comfort her like the routine of a game. I know it lulled me into a sense of false comfort. The routines we established between us broke down the feelings of strangeness, created a bond of familiarity.

We moved our chairs into a whole range of configurations. That too was part of the game. We could do anything in my office, I wanted her to see that, without real danger.

If I was Melinda's parent in the sense that she imagined me as a parent, I was also much of the time a fellow child with her.

When Melinda began to talk in our sessions, she talked non-stop, the words coming out in barrages like machine gun fire. She alternated between silence and prattle, the talk a disguised form of silence.

She sometimes talked to me as if she were talking out loud to herself.

In most of her relationships, Melinda felt herself to be the victim though in fact she tended to be the controlling one. She rarely allowed herself, despite her pretense that it was otherwise, to not be in control. A way to control situations, while at the same time not feeling responsible for her life, was to make herself appear to be a victim.

A victim needs a victimizer to complete the circle.

Melinda had been dating the same man for five years—she was twenty-three when she came to me—a man she complained about whenever his name came up in the conversation. He was insensitive to her feelings. She was repelled by much of his behavior and—this a recurrent obsession—his odor. The repulsion was uncharacteristic. Melinda was not ordinarily squeamish and was subject to few sexual taboos.

Why did she continue to see him if he repelled her?

She tended to ignore questions in areas of confusion or ambivalence, would take recourse in silence. It embarrassed her to admit there was any question she couldn't answer.

On the evidence, it appeared that she continued to see the man in order to complain of his failings. He was her occasion for grievance.

Sometimes she would say no more than a dozen words in an entire fifty minute session.

I didn't urge her to speak, not at first, not directly. I knew from our first meeting that to ask something directly of Melinda was to be denied. How did I know that?

"I want to be part of your life," she told me on one occasion. "I want you to think of me when I'm not here."

"Sometimes I do," I said. "I think of all my patients."

She mumbled something.

"What? . . . What?"

"It's cold in here, Yuri. Would you turn off the air-conditioning please. I'd appreciate it if you would consider my comfort once in a while."

"You sound as if you're talking to a servant," I said.

"I don't think you like me," she said. She had a sly smile on her face.

"If you don't think I like you, why are you smiling?"

Melinda pushed the corner of her lips down with her fingers. "Am I ugly?" she asked with a slight stammer.

"You haven't told me why you were smiling," I said.

"I wasn't," she said, covering her mouth with her hand.

When she took her hand away, her tongue shot out at me. "Are you angry? I don't want you to be angry with me." She raised her eyes which had been averted.

"You're a tease, Melinda," I said. "That makes people angry."

"Fuck you," she said, shouted it at me.

Her outburst, because it seemed so uncharacteristic— she had always been exceedingly polite in our sessions— shocked me. My first impulse was to order her out of the office—I wanted to punish her for offending me. "Fuck you," I said in return.

Her face broke. "I won't be talked to that way," she said. "You have no right to say that to me."

"You handled that very well, Melinda," I said.

She smiled joyously through her tears, wiped her cheeks with the back of her hand like a child. "Oh thank you," she said.

We moved in these sessions between war and seduction, different faces of the same aggression.

Her accounts of experiences with the man she referred to as her boy friend were unvaryingly unpleasant. It worried me that I was encouraging her to disparage him, that I had a personal stake in her negative feelings toward other men.

I mention my difficulties with Melinda to Adrienne who says, under her breath, that my misunderstanding of the girl is symptomatic.

I ask her to explain this unflattering description but she is in another room, her attention focused elsewhere. When I persist she says, "What do you really want?"

"Human contact," I say.

Adrienne laughs without amusement, laughs wryly, laughs with some measure of disdain.

Melinda protested again and again that I didn't like her, that it was only because I wanted her money that I continued to see her.

I tried different responses, admitted on one occasion that I sometimes found her unbearable. My remark brought a smile to her face, a look of triumph.

She denied that she was smiling.

We were facing each other that day at my insistence. The denied smile persisted brazenly.

Did I say that Melinda was seductive? Have I mentioned it anywhere?

"I wish I had a mirror so that I could show you your face," I said. "You continue to smile."

"You too," she said, her smile opening like a blossom.

I traced my lips with an imaginary finger. It was possible that our unacknowledged smiles mirrored one another.

I felt the strongest impulse to say something hurtful to her. My feelings must have expressed themselves in my face because she blanched, seemed almost to tremble.

"I have the feeling," she said, "that this is the beginning of the end of our relationship."

I was trembling, though I didn't know why, did and didn't. I was conscious of wanting to assure her that I had no intention of dropping her as a patient and conscious of withholding such assurance out of anger.

She turned her chair halfway around. "You want to be rid of me," she said.

"I'm your therapist not your lover," I said.

I had a dream about Melinda, a seemingly literal dream, not all of which I remembered. I wrote it down as soon as I awoke in a notebook I used to keep at bedside for just that purpose.

There is, I discover, only one chair in my office. The other chair, the patient's chair, is at some shop being reupholstered. Why hasn't it been returned? Melinda comes in conspicuously late, and asks indignantly where she is supposed to sit.

I offer her my seat. She remarks that I am still in it. It surprises me to discover that what she says is true. I am sitting in the very seat I offer her. It is wide enough for two, I say. At this moment, I'm not sure whether the ostensible patient is Melinda or Adrienne. She shakes her head coyly. I beckon to her with a finger. We are both standing. The chair is between us. It is not my office any longer but a bedroom, a room I had as a child. I point out the view from the window. The overgrown garden, the porcelain Cupids, the huge cherry tree just coming into blossom.

She says she admires the tree, though she is unable to believe that it actually produces cherries. Her breasts press against my back as she makes this announcement.

She says that the nipples of her breasts are real cherry buds.

I am leaning out the window trying to find a bud on the cherry tree to prove the tree's identity. There are no buds, only faded blossoms.

I bring in a handful of crushed petals. These are cherry blossoms, I say. Melinda giggles, says not really.

Just take my word for it, I say. This is a cherry tree. It produces sour cherries. I take a bud from the tree and hold it out to her.

She puts my fingers to her lips, says poor man. I notice that there is a red stain on the back of my hand.

I've always wanted to taste your blood, she says.

You're a liar, I rage. That's your blood. That's female blood.

Today was the fist time Melinda talked about her boyfriend, Phillip, by name.

She valued Phillip most when he ceased to be available. It was the pattern of their relationship. Melinda would mistreat Phillip, would reject and torment him until, provoked beyond endurance, he would stop seeing her. At that point she would decide that she was in love with him and plot obsessively to get him back.

When Phillip would return to her, as he did, she would feel contempt for him again as if such yielding were a failure of character. Any man foolish enough to love her was unworthy of her love.

I pointed this out to her, but for the longest time she refused to acknowledge it.

I tended to respond to Melinda's complaints about Phillip as if they were complaints about me.

As an aspect of this identification, I found myself intensely attracted to her. Was this counter-transference or something else?

Melinda told me of a dream in which I appeared in the guise of a teddy bear named Swoosh whom she held in her arms while she slept. That's all she offered of the dream.

I said the best way to remember dreams is to write them down as soon as she woke.

She pouted, said that most of her dreams were crazy and that it embarrassed her to think about them. The first three buttons of her gauzy blouse were open and I could see the lacy top of her pink undershirt. My impulse was to look away, but I didn't. I was almost certain she wasn't wearing a bra.

"I don't have to tell you my dreams if I don't want to," she said. "I have a right to privacy. Do you tell everything? I don't know anything about you, do I?" She turned her chair half way around to offer me a view of only half her face.

Her gesture enraged me out of all proportion. "I'm not going to let you do that," I said, getting to my feet.

"Don't you dare touch me," she said.

When I stood up she gasped as if in fright and shifted her chair part of the way back toward its original position.

"Put the chair back where it was or I'm going to discontinue the session," I said.

She grudgingly moved her chair back into position, sulked.

I returned to my seat with an assumption of dignity, felt relieved that she hadn't tested me further.

"Though I don't like it, Yuri, it's good for me to be treated that way."

"How do you feel I treated you?"

"Your face is flushed," she said. "Are you blushing?"

I repeated my question, had to repeat it several times to get a response.

"I don't understand what you're asking," she said.

"Tell me what's so funny," I said.

"I can't," she whispered, lowering her eyes. "I'll tell you when I know you better."

Our sessions had the quality on occasion of lovers' quarrels.

When I finally went to see Leo Pizzicati after several months of procrastination, I was in a state of intractable depression.

I sat down, somewhat disoriented, thinking myself in the wrong seat.

"Adrienne won't sleep with me," was the first thing I said, which was interesting because it was not what I had planned to say.

Leo seemed pained on my account, profoundly sad, which I immediately recognized as a projection.

I have the sense that I am making this up, recreating a scene out of a mix of memory and imagination. The ugly paintings on the wall, the tacky plastic furniture, the refusal to lay claim to style. There are a few inconsequential changes in his office (or maybe it's just a lapse of memory) but in matters that count nothing has changed.

I talk about Adrienne despite my intention to avoid that subject, get lost in a maze of evasion.

"I came to talk to you about a counter-transference problem I'm having with a woman patient," I say with about ten minutes left in the session.

"Are you fucking this patient?" he asks.

I laugh nervously at this abrupt perception, feel exposed and defensive. "I'm not fucking anyone," I say.

"Are you feeling sorry for yourself?"

I am close to tears, though unaware of feeling sad. "She wants me to fuck her," I say.

"And you can't turn her down?" he asks. "Does she have a name, this patient? Yuri, you look as if you want to cry."

I deny it, but the tears come in the wake of my denial. I refuse to cry, cover my face with my left hand, feel the tears prick my fingers. "Just a minute," I hear myself say.

I've never fully worked through the feeling that it is unmanly to cry so suffer embarrassment at breaking down. I remove my hand as if to say it's really nothing, a momentary aberration, but the crying continues and I am unable to speak.

When the fit is over, when I come back to myself, I begin to talk to Leo about my mother, though I have no new insights into that relationship. "What's the point of my telling you this?" I ask him.

He removes his pipe, says nothing, puffs coded messages in smoke.

I know the answer. My relationship with my mother is a paradigm of my relationship with all women. "My mother thinks I'm perfect," I say.

I should say something about that, not so much what I said to Leo, which is in a certain context, within a shared realm of assumptions, but say something about my mother, what she's like, how I experience her. Last week I lost her at the Metropolitan Museum of Art, couldn't find her for almost two hours. It is symptomatic. She had ways when I was a child of being there and not there. When she was missing we split up to search for her—Adrienne and Rebecca taking the first floor while I went upstairs. It was as if she had been claimed by some black hole. When she finally made herself available—she just seemed to appear—my mother refused to acknowledge that she had been lost. What I didn't mention to Leo was that while I was searching for her, I had the urge to take off and leave her to her disappearance. I felt—how should I put it—burdened by the pressure of her absence.

Two facts. My mother lost in the Egyptian tombs of the Metropolitan Museum. Melinda sitting with her back to me.

Sometimes in bed in the morning Adrienne would see something in my face and say, "What?"

I am wary these days with Melinda, take a distant and paternal tone in our sessions. She comments on my apparent disaffection, says it hurts her that I no longer care for her.

Her left breast is slightly higher than the right, I notice. The disparity touches me, takes my breath away.

Her new phase is less confrontational. She seems to court my sympathy, wants me to be pleased by the progress she is making.

Am I getting ahead of myself? I have fallen into disorder, have lost the thread of events.

It is another time. The question comes up at an unexpected moment. "Do you find me attractive?" she asks, looking sagely skeptical, aware of performance.

"What did I tell you the last time you asked?" I say.

"I can't trust your answer," she says, looking up shyly under hooded eyes. "How could you say no? I mean, you're trying to build up my sense of self-worth."

It is not what she says—do I even remember it as precisely as I pretend?—but the unspoken context we share.

I ask her if there's some way I can prove to her that I find her attractive.

The question enlists a sly smile and a delayed shrug. There are six minutes left in our fifty minute hour. I know that the next time we meet, which is two days from now, we will fuck. I have made an oblique offer and she has given oblique acceptance.

Reading over what I have written, I can see how melodramatic, even pathological, this all sounds. I knew what I was about to do was unethical and at the same time I felt driven to do it, felt the need to bust loose, to take what I had previously considered unacceptable risks. And maybe, said arrogance, in its nasty whisper, it would do us both some good.

I was resolved that it would happen once and once only, a demonstration of my attraction to her, and then we would use it as an area of exploration in her therapy. I have a predilection for being defensive so I will stop myself here to say that whatever the extenuating circumstances—I am imperfect, I am human—I am fully responsible for what happened with Melinda.

Outside of my professional commitments, I am a man of obsessive urges, sudden fixations, deep pockets of need. I have never learned to put off having the things I want. My tolerance for frustration is small. I sometimes, out of the blue, ache with undefined longing. Unaccountable things fill me with desire, present themselves as unavoidable needs. I barely slept the night before, was in a revved up state the next morning. Rebecca took note of it. "Daddy's in a silly mood," she said. Adrienne made an acerbic remark disguised as good natured teasing. "You used to be funnier," she said, withdrawing herself, fading out of the picture.

Having decided on a course of action, I gave my attention to logistics, the where and how of the matter. The idea of making love to her in my office, on the couch or on the rug, gave me pause. Yet I couldn't very well take her to a hotel without trashing the therapeutic situation altogether.

And then just before she was scheduled to arrive, I had a change of heart, decided not to pursue the matter further.

When she didn't show up on time—she was not usually late—I assumed she wasn't coming, assumed further that she had decided to break off treatment with me. I felt rueful.

I'm not very observant as to what women wear—it is the effect rather than the details that catch my attention—but I was aware that Melinda, when she made her belated entrance, was wearing a red dress with black trim. She didn't sit down, stood alongside her chair as if keeping it company. My sense of her was that she was glowing, that she was absolutely radiant.

I disguised my anxiety in exquisite self-possession. Her reality testing may have been weak in other circumstances, but Melinda understood my intentions in the full flower of their confusion.

There is no point in going on with this, in recounting how we got from here to there.

We used the seldom-used analytic couch for our transaction— I was glad to find some service for it—then spent what remained of the hour talking about what it was like.

It was like: good for me. Like that.

I remember her saying this much. "I feel, you know, that I've corrupted you."

With the putting on of my pants, I moved back into the role of therapist. "What makes you think you're so powerful," I said.

"I can get any man I want," she said, blushing. "I got you, didn't I?"

"Is that how it feels to you?"

"I feel used," she said. "I feel that you've taken advantage of me. I feel that you don't really like me. Not *really* like me. I feel that you shouldn't have done what you did. I feel that I've ruined everything. I'll never get well after this." Her eyes filled with tears.

I maintained an appropriate distance, performed my role as it suited me to perceive it.

The next three sessions followed a similar pattern. Melinda would arrive late, offer a perfunctory greeting, then lie down on the couch with her skirt above her knees. Although it had been my conscious intent not to continue the physical relationship, I didn't have the heart to deny either of us its melodrama. The sex was unexceptional, took place, we pretended, for the sake of the discussion in its wake.

What feelings did it excite? For me, it excited a sense of shame, a moderate not unbearable sense of shame. For Melinda: I no longer thought of Melinda's feelings as apart from mine.

I was collaborating with Melinda's fantasy, proving to her that she was capable of winning her therapist's (and father's) love. Can that be right? I am something of a literalist. I was not, despite the evidence of my behavior, lost to blind urge.

If I didn't stop this affair, it was because I didn't want to stop, was getting something from it that outweighed its disadvantages. It gave me a sense perhaps of power and accomplishment. Is that it?

I have the illusion that if I can say the right thing to Adrienne, she can't help but love me again or recognize (in that vast backwater of repressed feelings) that she hadn't stopped loving me. The words don't come, refuse to announce themselves, though the illusion itself sustains me.

I feel surges of passion for Melinda when she isn't there, particularly when she isn't there, my need for her compromised by her actual presence.

Melinda misses her appointment, leaves a garbled message with my answering service about some prior commitment. I feel vaguely needy the rest of the day, lack energy, doze during one of my sessions at the hospital. The patient, a lingerie fetishist, is so self-absorbed that I could put a mannequin in the room with him and he would go on with his obsessive story. Peter told me when he had an affair with a patient he felt so guilty he expected to be pulled out of bed at night—he once actually heard footsteps—and be carted off to jail.

I have a dream the next night of dying, wake in a state of grinding anxiety, barely able to breathe. I haven't felt this vulnerable since the early days of analysis—my first analysis. (First analysis=first love.)

Melinda comes in, coughing, huddled over, removes her scarf and coat and, without acknowledgement of me, begins to talk about an experience with her boy friend, Phillip. No reference is made to what's gone on the past three—three or four—sessions with us. It's as if I'm hardly in the room with her, as if she's talking in a dream.

I listen to her in an analytic way, try to pick up the real issue of the monologue. She is putting me in an intricate double bind. If I admit to feeling jealous, I lack the appropriate distance to deal with her problems, disqualify myself as her therapist. If I am not jealous, it indicates that I don't care for her sufficiently. My impulse is to pull down my pants and take her on the floor while she babbles on about Phillip's fear of making commitments.

"Why are you telling me this?" I ask.

She blinks her eyes in mock innocence. "What do you mean, Yuri? I don't understand what you're asking."

"You know very well what I'm asking," I say. "Something is going on with us that you're conspicuously avoiding."

She pouts childishly, flutters her hands. "Are you saying that all I can talk about here is you?"

"Melinda, why did you miss your last session?"

"I was sick," she says. "You'll say it's hysterical, I know, but the fact is I had a splitting headache. I almost didn't come today. I had to drag myself here. I just don't know what I'm doing here."

"Why did you come today?"

She shrugs, starts to say something and doesn't. "Because I'm in love with you," she whispers.

Leo has no answers for me, refuses to give advice, though I can tell from his face that he's worried about me. I can tell from the sorrowful pinch at the corner of his eyes that he suspects I am lost. I grieve for the person he sees.

"Another therapist couldn't have helped her as much as I have," I say.

His mouth moves into a smile that is gone the moment I perceive it. "You see the sex, do you, as part of a therapeutic program?"

"I no longer believe in therapy," I shout at him. "If I had any courage, I'd give it up and do something more honorable."

"Yes? What would you do? What is this honorable profession you have in mind for yourself?"

"If I gave up therapy," I say, "I think I'd give up psychology altogether."

"If you do, you do," he says, as if my defection from the science of the soul were not a serious issue.

Leo is unimpressed with my threat to give up the faith, and I am disappointed that he has no solace for me, come away from the session unimproved.

He doesn't tell me, as he might, that I am making a serious mistake. It is what I want from him and what he refuses to give me.

UPTOWN SHRINK CAUGHT WITH PANTS DOWN (Headline in The New York Post)

I was having difficulty sleeping through the night. I would wake periodically and look at Adrienne asleep or pretending to be asleep, turning in her sleep. I would move from back to side, from side to back, hoping to send tremors of my presence to her, to wake her to affection after this long sleep of rejection and denial. When I moved she also moved. When I turned toward her she would turn away as if there were some mechanism between us that had gone awry.

I looked at her sleeping form—her feigned sleep perhaps—and thought of the things I might do to her, was unable to separate the sexual from the violent. Pain short-circuited awareness. The moment I got in touch I was out of touch, lost to feeling, dead to myself. I imagined Adrienne in a fatal car crash, or crushed by the wheels of a train, or snuffed by a sniper's bullet, or falling from a high window. I suffered her loss, mourned her death as she slept next to me (or pretended to sleep) blissfully unaware. I was in a fever of madness.

I feel myself in some kind of helpless limbo, some deadly inertia. I talk to myself as though I were a robot. Move, I say. Sit. Eat. Stand. Right. Left. Turn. Move. Do something. Why aren't you moving? The answer is: I am. From outside and only from an exterior vantage is there the illusion of paralysis.

I go alone to the Virgin Islands for a week, a way of getting myself together, lie impatiently in the sun. I read detective stories and psychology journals, keep a fragmented record of my thoughts and feelings, interior dialogues, the story of my soul. It worries me that for seven days not once do I concern myself with the well-being of my patients. Melinda barely touches my consciousness. I consider at times not returning, going somewhere else, starting over. The truth is, I am homesick.

When I get back, Adrienne and Rebecca embrace me like a returning hero.

I feel a constant buzz of irritation in her presence as if

faced by unwanted news. We talk only to transact the business of the house, act as if the other were a moving shadow, a false image.

Melinda comes for another week, for two weeks, for three, seems eager to please, talks of the improvements in her life. I suggest that she see another therapist and, to my surprise and disappointment, she agrees without further discussion.

It is the same thing, the same experience, the same silent presence, the same oppressive house, the same feeling of hopelessness. Despite appearances, despite the extent of our dislocation, I am convinced that the deepest ties of feeling between us remain unbroken.

I decided to put down the story of my marriage as a means of investigating its peculiarly contemporary neurotic pattern. For months after Melinda leaves treatment with me, I feel the pull of her attraction—a tug on the sleeve of feelings from an invisible hand.

I made arrangements for her to see someone else, a therapist I knew only by reputation. She refused my choice.

After that she isn't available when I want her, except on rare occasions when she is, Melinda choosing the occasions. And then not at all. My need for her when she is not available is twice (is ten times) what it was when she was there for me.

She tells me in a letter that I was the best therapist she ever had. I am both amused and made anxious by the implications of the pun.

Eight

Beyond the Pleasure Principle

Routine helped me deceive pain. I took on new patients,
reentered therapy with my old therapist, read novels, did my
drawings, took a painting class one night a week, did things
with Rebecca. I seemed calm around the house. I don't think
anyone knew what was going on with me. Certainly not Yuri.
His face tortured with grievance.

Sometimes I took his face as a reflection of my own
condition. It was as if we were sharing the same sadness. (The
same office and the same feeling of loss.) That couldn't be
true.

When Carroway and I broke up I felt (what?) nothing.
I was broken up. I thought: it is all for the best. It is all for
the worst. I felt hurt, but didn't feel the pain. When I thought
about it calmly, I believed he would come back to me. He
loved me, didn't he? He valued me. There was a lesson to
Carroway's betrayal. There's always a lesson, isn't there? Men
are more emotionally frail than women. That's the moral of
all relationships between men and women. After all, we take
our houses with us.

Thomas was someone to talk to. He knew Carroway
(he had taught Carroway drawing at Pratt), he knew of our
relationship. He was one of the very few people either of us
had confided in. I don't think anyone else knew at the time

except Carroway's wife, Anna Marie. But that was something else. God, yes.

Carroway loves only himself, Thomas said. He helped me to understand what I already knew but refused to believe. That it was Carroway's pattern to evade intimacy. Thomas made himself available whenever I needed him. He never seemed to want anything for himself. (Eventually the bill will arrive, I thought.) How kind Thomas was. He was a good friend.

So I talked to Thomas about Carroway and later, when I felt I could trust him, about my drawings. This is what I realized. I realized that what I was getting from Thomas (we were not lovers then, that wasn't it) had replaced my need for Carroway. Then I asked myself, Why isn't there more between us? What does Thomas want from me? (I'm never really sure what people want from me.) The question I should have been asking myself is what do I want from Thomas. I tend to confuse what people want from me with what I want for myself.

I'm in session with a patient when Carroway calls out of the blue (he doesn't say who he is) and asks if we can get together. I know the moment I hear his voice that I no longer care in the same way. "I can't talk now," I say. "Can you call back in twenty minutes please?" My voice, which echoes in my ear, is calm. I am the professional person I pretend to be. (The hand holding the phone begins to cramp.)

"It gives me chills to hear your voice again," he says. "I love the sound of your voice."

"I'm with someone," I say. "Is there a number where I can reach you?"

"Look, I'll call back later," he says. "I don't want to impose myself on you while you have other commitments." He hangs up without the usual amenities.

I dismiss Sara Huddle a few minutes early. The woman has been locked for weeks in the same obsessional grievance. I am out of patience today, feel burdened by the tedium of her monologue. When she is gone, I try not to think about Carroway calling back. I have the sense that the entire psychoanalytic institute (Yuri among them) is observing my composure at this difficult time. I am a model of indifference. I take two Tylenol caplets for a headache that goes off and on like flashing neon lights. This is the drill: when he calls I will tell him that I don't want anything more to do with him. If he can't accept that, I would be willing to meet him very briefly in some public place to explain myself. Between patients, I rehearse my lines. I never get a chance to use them. Carroway doesn't call back.

After my last session I call Thomas and tell him of Carroway's disruptive call. Thomas is his concerned self. He says he will take off from work if I need to see him right away. I have an hour free at four Tomorrow, I tell him. He suggests that I come to his studio in Soho, but there really isn't time for that. Finally, we agree to meet, though postpone the decision of where. I sense we are involved in a tug of war.

I am lying down (coming down with something) and no one comes upstairs to ask how I am. (Even Rebecca stays away.)

I hear Yuri poking about in the kitchen, the shock waves of his presence. I want to scream something at him, some skyrocketing obscenity. (It is the thing about oppressors that they never identify themselves as oppressors.)

I feel crazed.

(Let me confess something. I have always been secretly afraid of losing touch. My most primitive terror is of coming apart. Going mad. There is little or no clinical evidence to support these feelings.)

I fall asleep briefly and Rebecca wakes me. "Are you coming down for dinner, mommy?"

"Only if I don't have to fix it," I say.

"Daddy's already made dinner." She says it, my lovely child, like a reproof.

"How could he?" I say. "There's nothing in the house."

I put on make-up, change my clothes (just my blouse really) and come down. Yuri has made pasta and meat sauce, has burned the garlic. Father and daughter have started eating without me.

"What's everyone been doing?" I say with worked-up cheer.

Yuri says something that makes no impression. Rebecca says, "Oh, Daddy!" with affectionate exasperation. I am thinking: How distant I feel from you, Yuri. It's as if your presence were an illusion on a TV screen. A lifelike configuration made up of inscrutable dots.

Yuri is in a good mood for a change. He jokes with Rebecca. I offer him a smile. I am thinking: Who's going to wash the pots and pans when dinner is over?

I have my sketchbook open in my lap. The drawing is already visualized, though the page remains blank. Yuri's presence (he is sitting across from me) makes it impossible for me to start. I know that he won't have the grace to leave (he knows I need to be alone) without my making a fuss.

We talk for a few minutes about the difficulty Rebecca is having with a math teacher. When our banalities exhaust themselves, I attend the blank page in my book. "Yuri, don't you have anything to do?" I ask in a kind voice. "You know I like to have time to myself after dinner."

He lets out one of his ponderous sighs. "I can't live like this, Adrienne," he says.

I find myself laughing crazily. "What do you think you want from me?" I ask. I hear Rebecca stir in her bed and I put my finger over my lips to caution him.

He raises his voice nevertheless. "You're not here," he shouts. "It's lonely living with an invisible woman."

"I don't want Rebecca to be brought into this," I say softly.

He jumps to his feet with a clamor, bumping the marble coffee table with his knee. An eruption is imminent. "I'm sorry about your knee," I whisper. "Think about it. There's really nothing I can do for you."

"What does your shrink think is going on?"

"I don't talk to Henry about you," I say. "As you're always telling me, you're not my problem."

"Your marriage of twelve years is going to hell," he says, his voice rising with each succeeding word, "and you don't talk to Henry about it. It's beyond belief. What the fuck do you talk to him about?"

I feel under siege. "I'm not prepared to discuss that with you," I say. "Okay?... Please don't wake Rebecca. She doesn't need to hear you run amok."

"You're maddening, you know? You drive me mad."

"So you like to tell me," I say, keeping my voice low. "You make yourself unhappy, Yuri, because you refuse to accept things as they are."

He points his finger at me as though it were a loaded gun. "What exactly do I refuse to accept?" The question reverberates through the house. His self-control is as fragile as egg shell. I imagine Rebecca sitting up in bed, listening in a terrified state.

"I don't want to have this conversation," I tell him. "I have a right not to have it if I don't want it."

I run upstairs to see if Rebecca is all right. She is sleeping restively, has kicked off one of her blankets.

(I am my own person, damn him.) I cover her, kiss her flushed cheek. "Love you, sweetie," I whisper.

I lie in bed for a while with the covers over my face, listening to the rasp of my breath. I have my hands (who can tell where hands will wander?) between my legs. I have trouble getting into it. The house is suddenly so quiet I can hear Rebecca's wheezy breathing from across the hall. And the sound of a television, the insinuating music of a suspense movie, from the house next door. I am wrapped up in depression like a mummy swathed in strips of sheet.

I reach my sister Grace on the phone and talk for almost an hour. (Yuri says two hours—I plan to check it when the bill comes in.) I end up telling her more of what's going on than I intend. It takes a while to unravel my story. And Grace has a story of her own.

Our mother has been calling her to complain about Spencer. Something is wrong with him and he absolutely refuses to see a doctor. She wants Grace to talk to him, which Grace thinks is funny. "I'd rather chew nails than ask anything of Spencer," she says. I laugh. Then Grace laughs. "I wasn't aware of being funny," she says, which makes us both laugh again. (I wonder why mother chose to call Grace and not me. I used to be the one she'd come to for advice.)

I tell her about Carroway's call at the office.

"You haven't tried to see him?" she asks. "That's not like you."

"I feel as if I can't bear not to see him," I say, "and other times it's as if it never really happened. (When I talk to Grace it's like talking to another version of myself.) Can you understand that? I worry about losing my own experience."

"I think I know where you're coming from," says Grace. "How's Yuri handling it?"

"He has very little reality for me these days."

"To tell you the truth," she says, "I've always had some problems with Yuri. Do you know what I mean? I think he comes on to me."

"I'm not sure I know what you mean," I say.

"I can't really explain," says Grace. "I feel like, you know, he can't tell the difference between us."

Yuri is occupied watching a movie on television when I come back downstairs. I say "Hi" and he smiles in delayed reaction.

The movie is a Hitchcock film called "Marnie," which I had seen pieces of on television before. (Whenever I watch, Marnie seems to be on horseback, the horse out of control.)

During a commercial he asks who I had been talking to for almost two hours. I see no reason not to tell him. "It was Grace," I say. "My mother is worried about my step-father's health." Yuri mumbles something. I feel calmer, sit down on the couch and do a drawing, a self-portrait with half the face blurred out. We have returned to our routine of silence. After his movie is over, Yuri says goodnight, looks over at me, expecting something (what, Yuri?) and goes upstairs. "Sleep well," I say to him. I feel tender toward him in his impending absence.

When you no longer love someone it is hard to remember how it was when you did.

In the office we share I come upon a notebook of Yuri's which contains journal entries of the past year. I open the book on a sudden urge, intrigued with what's going on with him. I stop to read certain passages in which my name appears or the names of other women are mentioned. He has not been so innocent. A line strikes me. "I am in mourning for an object which is itself in mourning." I repeat the sentence to myself.

It is five minutes past midnight when I phone Carroway from the office. He answers in a harsh voice on the second ring. "I'm sorry if I woke you," I say in a whisper. "Who the fuck is this?" he says, shouts. (As if I were making an obscene phone call.) I hang up, then moments later call again. I am in a state, my heart flapping wildly, though also in control. This time he answers on the first ring, says in a muffled voice, "What do you want?" "So you knew it was

me," I say. "I don't expect to be treated this way from a...."
The sentence doesn't end.

"Why don't I call you back first thing in the morning,"
he says.

"I want to talk now."

"I think it would be better if I got back to you in the
morning," he says. "Good night, sir."

"Anna Marie is in the room, I suppose."

"That's an intelligent assumption. Good night."

"Do you ever think of me?" I ask.

"I'm going to have to hang up now," he says. "Okay?"
I say nothing, wait for the axe.

"Get some sleep," he says and is gone.

I feel nothing. I am afraid to open myself to whatever
I am really feeling. When I turn around there's Yuri, in the
dark blue silk bathrobe I had once given him for his birthday,
watching me from the doorway. "Do you want something?"
I ask him. There is a rash on his forehead that extends almost
to the bridge of his nose.

I want to know who you were talking to on the phone,"
he says in a voice full of childish belligerence.

"It doesn't concern you," I say cooly.

"If I'm concerned, it concerns me," he says. He has his
hands on his hips and sways slightly as he talks.

He is angry enough to smash me, I sense, though I feel
no danger. He'll be sorry if he lays a hand on me. That's what
I'm thinking. "Come off it, Yuri," I say to him.

He repeats his demand, takes a step in my direction.

"It will only hurt you to know," I say. "Do you think I
want to hurt you? I don't want to hurt you."

"And Nixon is not a crook," he says. "I think you get off
on hurting me." His face looks as if the skin had been scraped
with sandpaper.

"I have my own problems," I say. "I'm not going to be
sucked into yours." I walk past him in the narrow space to

show him I am not afraid of him. He brushes me with his shoulder.

He waits until I am past him, until I begin to climb the steps, before shouting my name. "Have the decency not to throw your shit in my face," he says.

"You think I'm indecent, Yuri?" I ask the question without turning around. My legs ache. I am aware suddenly of being exquisitely tired. "Is that what you think of me, Yuri?"

He follows me up the basement stairs into the living room before answering. "That's the kindest way it might be put," he says.

"Say what you mean, you mother fucker." I keep my voice down, focus my anger.

"I didn't get that," he says.

"I'll tell you something, Yuri," I say. "If you saw a movie about our lives," I say, "you'd find me the more sympathetic character. You know that's true."

He shakes his head in denial, looks lost. "Anything is possible," he says, "in a medium that means to deceive. As a matter of fact, Adrienne, you're full of shit."

I have the sense of being an observer of some obscene public event. I am watching an ugly domestic squabble in the movies in which someone like myself is a major participant, a crazy fight to the death has just begun, a fight that will get uglier and uglier until it breaks off into something else, some vulgar and painful resolution, and I watch myself think, No, I don't want this, and I hold up my hand like a traffic cop. I witness myself holding up my hand. "I don't want to talk now, Yuri. Okay?" I disengage.

He follows me up to the bedroom, stares his anger at me for a long time without saying a word. It doesn't frighten me. There isn't anything he can do to frighten me.

"Yuri, if you have something to say, say it. What do you want?"

He turns around, returns downstairs.

It is a relief to be free of him. I make a bet with myself that he will return (I know him too well) in five maybe ten minutes for a final flail. There will be an unfelt apology or a last angry word. I put off going to sleep.

I am wrong as it turns out, but not very far wrong. (I know Yuri. I can set my watch on his heart beat.) At breakfast the next morning, he leans over to me and says he is sorry about last night. Rebecca is at the table so I merely nod in acknowledgement

Later, as he is leaving the house, I say, "You don't need to apologize to me for anything, Yuri."

He nods, offers me the trace of a smile. "I think I apologize to you because I want you to apologize to me," he says.

"I think I know that about you," I say.

Yuri goes out, closes the door behind him. Before I can sit down to my second cup of coffee, he is back.

His hair is in disarray even though he has been outdoors less than a minute. "I feel patronized by you," he says. "That's all I want to say."

"Let's not have another fight," I say. "Okay?"

"What else is there?" he says. "It's the only contact left us."

"Please don't shout," I whisper. "At least close the door, honey. You know how I feel about public scenes."

"Whenever I say something you don't want to hear, you accuse me of shouting," he shouts. "The neighbors are in the audience watching the movie of your life. Show them how sympathetic you are."

"I'm not angry at you now," I say. I squeeze his hand. "I was thinking last night that you're not so bad." I can feel my face flush.

He puts his arm around my waist, pulls me to him.

"You'll be late, honey," I say. I have to push him gently toward the door to get him out.

When he is gone I feel safe again. There is more air to breathe. I think of clearing up the kitchen (Yuri has left his coffee cup in the sink), go upstairs to take a shower instead. (I don't think of Carroway's call.) While I wash my hair, I imagine myself watching the movie of our life. It is not our real story. And there are distractions. I hear Yuri's key rattling in the lock. He is always there, waiting to get in.

Nine

The Movie of Their Lives

An overhead shot of Brooklyn Heights at dusk. We see the Brooklyn Bridge, the setting sun glancing off it like veils of light. The camera moves through the various rooms of an elegantly furnished Brooklyn Heights brownstone, stopping to rest in an upstairs bedroom, where we catch a man and woman (in their early forties) in the act of making love, the door slightly ajar, a child's eye at the open slit. The eye recedes as we approach it, disappears altogether. You never say anything, the woman whispers. How do I know what you feel?

An immaculately dressed, dour man, wearing turned down hat and dark glasses, studies the two brass plaques on a front wall of the same brownstone. The camera moves in by degrees on the signs: Yuri A. Tipton, Psychotherapist, and under the first, Adrienne French-Tipton, Psychotherapist. The man looks behind him before entering the building, wary of being observed.

A phone is ringing inside the house. Adrienne and Yuri answer virtually at the same time on different extensions. The call is from the assistant producer of a midnight television talk show, inviting them to appear on a program dealing with the issue of highly successful husbands and wives in the same profession. Adrienne says maybe, she needs to think it over. A decision is deferred. Yuri is adamant, says he is opposed to cheapening their professional lives by making them the occasion of situation comedy. They get into a heated argument disguised as civilized discussion. The debate ends without resolution, with Adrienne going downstairs to see a patient. The camera watches her descent as if it were a trip into a nether world.

The patient is the man we saw outside the building, a Long Island real estate developer named Brian Carroway. Carroway, as he calls himself, has come through the referral of a colleague, and although Adrienne's time is already oversubscribed, she has agreed to this preliminary interview out of professional courtesy. Carroway has a disarmingly open manner. His style is to insinuate intimacy, to presume on an implicit understanding between himself and his listener. He and his wife, he tells Adrienne, have an open marriage in which each is free to explore the sensual life so long as the integrity of their marriage is not otherwise violated. His most recent affair has been with a eighteen year old McCrory's sales girl, who chews gum during the sexual act, which Carroway says has been a near-religious experience for him.

His problem is that his wife, Anna Marie, has stopped confiding her experiences to him. As a consequence, he has become jealous and has begun to spy on his wife. He suspects, he says, that Anna Marie actually prefers one of her lovers to him, though he is yet to discover which one. While he makes his confession, almost as a form of punctuation, Carroway flirts with Adrienne.

We see at the same time (on split screen) Adrienne talking to Carroway and Adrienne talking to Yuri about her session with Carroway. Composing herself, Adrienne says to Carroway that maybe he ought to explore the need to share the details of various loveless sexual encounters.

Yuri advises Adrienne not to take on Carroway as a patient. Before Carroway leaves, he praises Adrienne for her perceptiveness, claiming that he feels, on the basis of this first session, already greatly improved. He's a sexual exhibitionist, says Yuri, which is why he wants a woman therapist. Adrienne says the problem has a certain case study quality that interests her, and that she intends to have another exploratory session with Carroway.

Yuri tell Adrienne that he has been having problems with a young woman who, in a transference reaction, has confided that she is in love with him. Is she a temptation? Adrienne asks, half jokingly. To which Yuri says in a deadpan, It's all I can do to resist her.

We cut to Yuri sitting opposite his doting patient, Margo Goldhart, in the same office in which we had seen Adrienne and Carroway. Margo says it is difficult for her to say but the fact is she is disappointed with her therapist, glancing at Yuri slyly to see what impact her remark has made. When Yuri doesn't respond, she escalates the terms of her attack. Let me say, Yuri says, that I don't think either of us believes I'm the real cause of your anger. How awful you must think I am? she whispers. Their session has the quality of a lovers' quarrel.

The scene dissolves into one in which Adrienne and Carroway are facing each other in the same office. Carroway tells Adrienne that he has put together a dossier of his wife's deceptions, neglecting his business and his health in the process. He has learned, he says, that Anna Marie is having a serious affair with either a politician or a psychologist. Carroway picks up his reflection in an ornamental mirror on the wall. He watches himself cry. I hate my life, he says. It's a strain to keep up pretenses. You know what I'm saying?

Adrienne nods. If the way you live gives you pain, Carroway, it might make sense to try something else, she says. No?

It's important for me to hear that, Carroway says. You're good for me, Dr. Tipton.

When he leaves, Adrienne remains in her seat, staring at the vacated chair.

We notice Carroway hanging around the Tiptons' brownstone after his session is over. Yuri passes him; the men take each other's measure.

The camera picks up Adrienne and Yuri having dinner together in their formal dining room. Yuri is saying if Adrienne wants to do it, he'll do the television show with her. Adrienne says she still hasn't made up her mind on the issue. Their 11 year old daughter, Rebecca, comes in, wanting to know if her parents have any objection to her smoking grass, just a little to see what it's like, with her best friend Dora. Absolutely no, honey, Adrienne says. Yuri says he thinks it would be a good idea if Rebecca waited until she was a little older. How much older? Rebecca asks. Thirty years older, says Yuri. After Rebecca has gone, Yuri says maybe they ought to take her out of the progressive private school she's in and put her in a more traditional place where they don't start smoking marijuana until they're twelve. Adrienne says she trusts Rebecca to make the wise choice. I think she's wonderful too, Yuri says.

When Yuri asks if Carroway has gotten easier to deal with, we cut to Anna Marie and Carroway at a more elaborate table in another dining room, sniffing cocaine. Carroway kisses the palm of his wife's hand as she studiously inhales, Anna Marie looking off with sultry indifference into the distance. What's going on? he asks. When she doesn't answer, he bends back one of her fingers. Don't, she says.

We cut back to Yuri and Adrienne, their images superimposed over Carroway and Anna Marie. Carroway is one of the most open people I've ever met, Adrienne is saying. It's a deceptive mode, Yuri says. The man's manipulative.

Through the use of montage, we see Yuri meet with a succession of patients, repeating himself, striking similar attitudes again and again. At some point there is a changing of the guard, Adrienne descending the steps to the office as Yuri goes upstairs to the apartment. He stops to give her a hug. What's this? she says.

Walking to his car, Yuri is approached by Anna Marie, who apparently has been waiting outside the building for him. Are you Dr. Tipton? she asks him. He asks her which Dr. Tipton she wants. Whichever one you are, she says.

We see Anna Marie sitting next to Yuri as they ride along in his silver nondescript Japanese car. Anna Marie does the talking while Yuri listens or gives the illusion of listening. Anna Marie tells him some "facts" about Carroway she thinks he ought to know. Carroway has worked for the diplomatic corps and the CIA—she calls it by a code name—has sold arms and smuggled drugs, has beaten her. She opens her blouse to show him a bruise on the side of a breast. She insists that her husband, though appearing to be gentle, is a violent and dangerous man. We notice that someone in a red sports car appears to be following them.

What has Carroway told you about me? she asks.

Not a thing, says Yuri. What has he told you about me?

He doesn't admit to seeing a psychiatrist, she says. I found your name in his address book. I came to see you so you wouldn't get the wrong idea about me. I'm probably what you would call an abused homemaker.

That's not a phrase in my vocabulary, says Yuri.

As a result of Carroway's abuse, she reports, she has developed a heart-shaped rash in the vaginal area. The presence of this rash, for which she feels no personal responsibility, embarrasses her.

Yuri declines her offer to witness the embarrassing rash with his own eyes.

We cut to Anna Marie sitting in Yuri's class while he delivers a lecture on "The Problem of Transference in the Therapeutic Process." Afterwards, they have a drink together at a local bar called The Class Act. What's going on between us? Yuri asks.

I've come to see you about my husband's therapy, she says, wide-eyed. Is there something wrong with that?

You know of course, he says, that Carroway's in therapy with my wife and not with me.

Adrienne is in her office, writing something in a notebook. A knock at the door startles her and she closes the book and puts it back in a drawer. Carroway comes in and takes his seat without a word of acknowledgement. He is on this occasion even more morose than usual. Adrienne studies him. The camera focuses on Carroway's impassive face, his expression masked by dark glasses.

What is it, Carroway? she asks.

Your husband doesn't want you to be my therapist, he says.

I make my decisions independent of my husband, she says. And you have no way of knowing what my husband thinks.

I have my sources, he says.

Later in the hour, Carroway says that Anna Marie confided to him that Yuri is one of her lovers.

You told me another time that she makes things up, Adrienne says. Why do you believe her now?

I've seen them together, Carroway says.

I don't believe you, Adrienne says.

When Carroway leaves, the camera follows him out the door to a red sports car parked in front of the building.

We cut to Adrienne going through the drawers of Yuri's desk. In one she finds a matchbook from a restaurant she has never been to. She sits in the patient's chair, staring into space as if consulting her other self.

We cut to Anna Marie presenting herself at the receptionist's desk at a hospital clinic as Yuri's wife. Yuri is annoyed when he discovers her in his office waiting for him, says the clinic is for patients who can't afford to see him in his private practice.

I wouldn't have come if it wasn't important, she says in her breathless way. Carroway thinks he knows something about us. He's been making a lot of wild threats.

I assume you told him there was nothing between us, he says.

She shakes her head. If you deny something to Carroway, she says, it has the effect of making him believe it more. The best thing to do is ignore him when he gets into his jealous rages. Besides, he may know something, if you get my drift, that we don't know.

I have no intention of giving your husband cause to worry, Yuri says. I am a man who happens to believe in marital fidelity.

They are kissing when a black teenager, Yuri's next patient, walks in on them.

Leaving the clinic, Yuri hears what sounds to him like a gun shot and throws himself to the ground. He is helped to his feet by two older women, both a little potted, who advise him to go home and sleep it off.

We cut to Adrienne concluding a call from the kitchen phone to a former therapist. I feel I'm in some kind of trouble, she is saying. Yuri is whistling to himself as he comes in on her. Tuesday is fine, she says and hangs up the phone.

Happy about something? she says to Yuri, her anger only thinly disguised.

As a matter of fact, I'm feeling fairly down, babe, Yuri says.

Adrienne shakes her head in ironic wonder. It's usual to whistle, I suppose, when you feel down. Of course, when you feel happy what you do is cry, right?

It takes two to make an argument, Yuri says, walking away.

Adrienne shouts after him, Don't you just know everything.

We see Adrienne talking to her daughter Rebecca, who is sprawled out on the living room floor, doing her homework. There's something I feel I have to tell you, she says. Rebecca puts her hands over her ears. What is it? she asks.

Yuri and I are having some problems, she says. It's

nothing really. I just want you to understand where the tension you feel comes from. I'm not telling you anything you don't know.

I hate it when you and daddy are having problems, Rebecca says. I hate problems. I hate the word problems. Adrienne hugs Rebecca. The camera holds them in embrace then fades to black.

Yuri and Adrienne, facing forward as if posing for separate pictures, are riding in an elevator. They stand a foot or so apart, avoid looking in the other's direction, are almost synchronized in their isolation. They come into the large high-ceilinged apartment of their friends, Peter and Barbara Cohen. A largish party is in progress. We discover, by overhearing conversations, that all the guests are therapists or companions of therapists. Shop talk abounds.

After embracing Yuri and Adrienne, Peter says that he heard they were about to become television celebrities, that they were going to tell the world how they handle their feelings of rivalry and competition. Joking aside, Adrienne says, Yuri and I are supportive of one another. When Peter asks if they're actually going to do the TV show, Yuri says most likely; Adrienne says absolutely not. Their audience laughs. Yuri and Adrienne stare at each other in mute anger.

Yuri is in the coat room—the master bedroom—looking at a painting on the wall when Barbara comes up from behind and asks him what he thinks. He kisses Barbara on the cheek. You're looking very sexy tonight, he says. You look a little like what's her name, the movie actress who's been rediscovered. I'm thinking of. . . He closes his eyes. My memory is failing me. Louise Brooks.

Barbara, blushing, gives Yuri a hug. That's very nice, she says, though I don't really know who Louise Brooks is.

In the next room, we spot Adrienne talking with great animation to a man with prematurely white hair. I read in "The New York Review," she is saying, that we are living in a time of post- civilization. I just figured out what that really means. It means we live in a time when a divorce lawyer makes twice as much as a therapist.

Maybe he's providing a better therapeutic service, he says.

Only a lawyer would say that, she says.

We see Adrienne edging through the crowd, her nervous smile like a flickering light.

We cut to Rebecca's bedroom, see her writhing in her sleep. She lets out a cry, bolts into sitting position. Her eyes still closed, she brushes an imaginary bug from her face. A teenaged baby-sitter (her boyfriend a step behind her) rushes into the room. They are both disheveled, partially undressed. Rebecca opens her eyes, squirms. You're having a bad dream, the sitter says.

Adrienne comes out of the bathroom in her nightgown. We follow her into the bedroom where Yuri is sitting up in bed waiting for her. I'm really tired, she says. Can we hold off this talk you've been pushing on me until tomorrow?

You were the sexiest woman at the party, Yuri says. When I saw you from across the room, I said to myself that's the woman I should have married.

Adrienne gets under the covers, pretends to drift into sleep. Yuri lies stiffly on his back, eyes closed, eyes open, eyes closed again, hours of discontent pressed into a minute. Adrienne, who is not sleeping after all, turns on her side toward him. Will you hold me? she asks in a child's voice. I don't want sex. I just want to be held.

Yuri says okay under his breath.

Yes? she asks.

You can always lie with me, he says. Fade to black.

Carroway is in therapy session with Adrienne. If we met under other circumstances, he says, at a party or something, would you have found me attractive?

I don't see any use in taking this any further, she says.

If you really want to help me, says Carroway slyly, why stop short of doing the very thing that might help me the most?

Adrienne laughs at that, says, Since when has sex solved anything in your life?

It's the final solution, he says.

Later in the session, Adrienne says, I can see this is not going to work out. I could give you the names of some other therapists, people I'd be willing to recommend.

That's exactly it, Carroway says, getting out of his chair. Do you see what the bitch is doing to us?

We cut to Yuri getting out of his car at the hospital parking lot. Noticing Anna Marie waiting for him at the main entrance, Yuri goes around the block and into a side door. When he gets to his office, she is waiting for him in the anteroom.

She lifts her hair and shows Yuri a bruise on the side of her face. If Carroway did that, Yuri says, leave him. She says she wants to move out but is afraid to take the step, that Carroway has threatened her. He has also threatened to hurt Yuri, she says, if he finds them together. Yuri says he'll talk to her later.

Leaving the hospital, Yuri discovers Anna Marie leaning against his car as if posing for a fashion photograph. She pleads with him to go with her to get her things—she wants to move out—and though Yuri says he doesn't have time, we see him driving her to her house in Port Washington.

I'm sure Carroway's not home, she says. Today's his day at his studio.

We see Yuri accompany Anna Marie to the door of her designer suburban house. As she unlatches the door, Carroway emerges from the other side of the house and invites Yuri in at gun point.

Yuri says he has to get back to his office to see patients.

Think of this as a house call, says Carroway.

In the interview that follows—Carroway and Yuri face each other in a parody of the therapeutic situation—Carroway alternates between insinuating geniality and righteous anger. Anna Marie sits in a neutral corner reading a magazine apparently unconcerned with the discussion. What Carroway wants, it becomes apparent, is to watch Yuri and Anna Marie make love so as to validate his suspicions. Yuri deflects the offer by pretending not to understand it, tries to cajole Carroway into giving up his gun.

Without looking up from her magazine, Anna Marie says, Why not give the asshole what he wants and get it over with.

When Yuri moves toward the door, Carroway fires a shot just over his head.

I want to get this straight, Yuri says, taking a seat. Am I to understand that you would kill a man for not going to bed with your wife?

Carroway says, I have no problem with that. Yuri says that he needs privacy for sex, that it wouldn't work for him with Carroway watching them.

Pointing the gun at Yuri's head, Carroway says that no Long Island jury would convict a man for killing an intruder in his own house.

Anna Marie comes over and sits down on Yuri's lap. There is a mix of rage and fascination on Carroway's face.

Why don't you make love to Anna Marie while I watch? Yuri says.

The idea intrigues Carroway momentarily, but then he rejects it, shaking his head regretfully. She'd rather make it with you, he says.

Yuri asks Anna Marie if what her husband says is true. It's best to play along with him when he's like this, she whispers. She puts her arms around Yuri's neck and kisses him open-mouthed. Punctuated by a groan of rage, Carroway picks up a ceramic ashtray and flings it against the wall, missing Anna Marie and Yuri by no more than a foot. Anna Marie gets up and rushes into the bathroom, locking the door behind her.

That concludes our session for today, Carroway says, putting the gun away in his jacket pocket. I'll tell you I feel a whole lot better now.

Before Yuri leaves, Carroway gives him a bottle of champagne as a token of apology. No hard feelings? he asks. Yuri reluctantly shakes his hand. Have a drink with me, Carroway says.

Yuri says he has to get back, has appointments to keep.

In the manner of a host escorting a friend, Carroway walks Yuri to his car. He apologizes again, is profuse in his regrets. Drive carefully, he says.

As Yuri drives away, the camera peers through a side window of the Carroways' house. The room seems empty at first, then we discover Carroway and Anna Marie locked in sexual embrace under the piano.

Adrienne has completed clinic and is walking toward the subway when she sees Carroway coming toward her.

What are you doing here? she asks.

He looks around him as if wary of being observed. I have a loft space a few blocks from here where I make sculpture, he says.

Adrienne nods, starts to move on, stops herself. I don't believe you, she says. I think you were waiting for me.

Carroway offers to bet her ten dollars that he is telling the truth, offers her ten to one odds.

We see them walking through the local streets, arriving at a seemingly deserted industrial building. Adrienne nervously follows him up three flights of stairs, stands behind him, fascinated, as he unlocks the door.

We see the disbelief on Adrienne's face as they enter the loft space. There are sculptures around the room in various media—pop art assemblages of a marginally competent if imitative sort. The room is sparsely furnished: a couch, a love seat, two wooden chairs, a plexiglass table. We see the scene through Adrienne's eyes. On the single upper level, there is an elegant spiral staircase leading to an open room with a kingsize bed.

All right, she says, you have the key to this place, but how do I know you've done these sculptures.

In the next scene, we see them at the table, drinking wine out of the same glass. And then we see her following Carroway up the spiral stairs to the bedroom.

I don't know what's going on, Adrienne says, sitting down on the bed. I really don't know why I'm here.

You wanted to see for yourself, Carroway says. And you want to get even with your husband.

We match dissolve to Yuri and Adrienne sitting opposite each other in their living room, each with a glass of white wine in hand. They have been discussing their problems for several hours and seem to have run out of things to say.

A robbery is going on in a house directly across the street. We cut away from Yuri and Adrienne's conversation to the scurrying of figures on a roof. Two police cars drive up and double park in front of the Tiptons' house. The two policemen in the first car get out and, after some apparent confusion as to where to go, head toward Yuri and Adrienne's door.

Yuri, looking burnt out, is bent forward on the couch, his hands pressed together. Adrienne, he says, you're so goddamned involved in the minute vibrations of your soul, that you never see anything as it really is.

Yuri, if you saw a movie of our life, Adrienne says—I thought about this this morning at breakfast—you would find me the more sympathetic character.

Yuri thinks about this, seems to envision such a movie, admits that Adrienne might be right. If that were so, he says, it would only go to prove the deceptiveness of cinematic illusion.

Two policemen emerge from the house across the street with a young black man between them, his hands in cuffs. A handful of onlookers applaud. This is a terrible mistake, the prisoner says. I was the one being robbed.

We cut to Yuri and Adrienne getting dressed to appear "live" on the Norman Safflower midnight talk show. Adrienne changes her clothes several times, unable to decide what she wants to wear. She asks Yuri which of two outfits he prefers. He chooses the more conventional one, and Adrienne decides to wear the other. That was my real choice, Yuri says.

In a taxi going to the television studio, Yuri takes Adrienne's hand. He kisses her. Is this a terrible mistake we're making, baby? she asks. We'll do fine, he says. We see Adrienne and Yuri, in makeup, waiting backstage at the television studio for their entrance. The make-up transforms them; they look as if actors are impersonating them. An obsequious woman briefs them on the format of the show. Wives and husbands will be separated for the first part of the program, and interviewed independently. In the second part, they get to discuss each other's "input" face to face. Yuri objects, says that no one told them they would be required to answer questions apart from each other.

I refuse to go through with this, Adrienne says.

We cut to Carroway and Anna Marie watching the Norman Safflower show on a large color television. Safflower, a distinguished looking white-haired man with an unusually resonant voice, is on screen introducing his guests. The guests (a pair of tennis pros, a brace of lawyers, and Yuri and Adrienne) seem barely visible next to the charismatic presence of the host. What we are dealing with tonight,

Safflower intones, is the innate competitiveness of the male animal and the female animal. The camera pans the faces of each of the subjects (as Safflower calls them), the women first, Adrienne averting her eyes. From a long shot, we discover that husbands and wives are seated on opposite sides of a revolving stage.

The women are interviewed first. The silken-tongued Safflower wants to know how they would compare their own competence in their respective fields to that of their husband's.

The camera is on Adrienne, who seems frozen momentarily, unable to get out a word. She smiles nervously, opens her mouth without sound. Safflower repeats the question, says not to worry she is among friends. Looking away, Adrienne says that she and Yuri are equally competent, that their strengths lie in different areas, that she's a better technician but that his intuitive gifts are greater.

But you do feel you're the better technician? Safflower asks. Do you think your husband would agree to that judgment?

We get the gist of the program through a succession of brief takes. Prodded by Safflower, Yuri says at one point, I have no intention of deprecating Adrienne's abilities, which are considerable, but much of what she knows she's learned from me.

The show turns into a nightmare for the participants, though they pretend for the most part—Yuri and Adrienne the exception— to be amused by the conflict the moderator generates.

In the second half of the show, husbands and wives face each other across a table. The hostility has become almost tangible. The male lawyer says, as if a joke, that his wife has the sense of high purpose of a Madame de Farge. When she picks up her knitting, I confess I get a little nervous.

Well, she says, looking at her husband—the camera moving between them—I don't wittingly defend violators of the public trust. And I won't sacrifice the truth as I know it just to get a client off.

Adrienne says at one point—He may have taught me everything he knows, but I've already forgotten whatever that was.

In the taxi going home from the television studio, Yuri and Adrienne are so furious with each other they can barely speak. This was your idea, Adrienne says.

They bump shoulders going into the house and face each other like lifelong enemies.

I've known all along that there are other women, she says.

You don't even know who you are, he says.

When Yuri returns after taking home the sitter, Adrienne has his suitcase packed and waiting for him. He goes up to the bedroom, ignores Adrienne who is pretending to sleep, and repacks in a white heat, throwing the clothes his wife had given him across the room. Before leaving the house, Yuri goes into Rebecca's bedroom and lingers, sitting on his suitcase next to the bed.

We see Yuri leave the house with his suitcase, walk into a local upscale bar, and order a Scotch with water. A woman comes over and sits down next to him; she introduces herself as a former patient.

We cut to Adrienne getting undressed—she has been under the covers in her clothes—in a kind of dazed slow motion. She is lying in bed with the lights on, dozing, when the phone rings. You woke me up, damn you, she says to whoever it is. A woman's voice asks to speak to the other Dr. Tipton.

Yuri's not here, Adrienne says. Who the hell is this?

Anna Marie identifies herself, says she has left Carroway and needs someone to talk to.

You're not thinking of doing something desperate? Adrienne asks.

I don't understand what you're asking, Anna Marie says. What do you mean by something desperate?

We next see Adrienne in the bathroom taking a couple of valium, and then curled up on the living room couch reading a magazine.

Adrienne is just beginning to doze off on the couch when the doorbell rings. At first she is afraid to answer, then she picks up a poker from the fireplace and goes to the door.

Anna Marie appears and identifies herself. Adrienne steps aside and lets her in. She looks for a place to put the poker she has been holding behind her back.

Some time has passed. The two women are sitting on the couch, talking with a certain ease.

Carroway gets off on women who are smarter than he is, says Anna Marie. He thinks of sex as an educational experience.

We cut to Yuri sitting on a couch in Peter and Barbara Cohen's living room. Barbara sits across from him in an oversized bathrobe.

I'm writing a novel, she says, about my own tattered marriage in the disguise of Adrienne's and your marriage. You're the first person I told this to. I hope you feel privileged. If you want to go to sleep just say so and I'll go away.

I'll take a hotel room tomorrow, Yuri says. I don't think I'll get to sleep tonight. Look, don't feel you have to entertain me, Barbara.

I'm going to fix myself one more drink and then go to sleep, she says. An hour later they are still talking.

We cut to a shadowy figure standing sideways at the entrance to the Tiptons' house. He knocks twice. We hear Adrienne's voice asking who's there.

It's me, Carroway says.

Adrienne opens the door just enough to make herself heard. What do you think you're doing here? she says.

We hear Anna Marie in the background saying, Don't let him in.

Adrienne, I want you to know there's nothing to be frightened of, he says.

Whenever someone says something like that to her, Adrienne says, she wants to run for her life.

Carroway tries to charm his way by her, promises that he will only stay a few minutes.

Do you have any idea what time it is? Adrienne asks and starts to close the door. Carroway forces his way in.

Adrienne blocks his way, says that if he tries to go by her, she'll call the police. Carroway clamps his hand over mouth. I thought you liked me, he says. He presses her up against the wall and tries to kiss her. She kicks him in the leg.

I want you to leave, she says. I mean it.

Your husband's not here, is he? he says in an insinuating voice. Do you know why he's not here? I think you know without my spelling it out.

He decides to leave and does.

When Adrienne returns inside, Anna Marie is no longer there. Adrienne goes down the steps to her office. The outside entrance to the office is unlocked and it seems evident that Anna Marie has gone. Adrienne bolts the door and curls up on the therapeutic couch. She hears footsteps and jumps to her feet. Go away, she says. Rebecca comes into the room. She is crying. Where is everyone? she says. Mother and daughter cuddle together on the couch, arms around each other.

We cut to Yuri who wakes with a start. He is on a couch in the Cohen's living room. It takes him a while to determine where he is. He climbs over Barbara, who is asleep on the rug, buttons his shirt, searches the living room floor for his shoes. We next see him riding down alone in the elevator, combing his hair with his hand.

Yuri is crossing a street when a red sports car appears from nowhere and almost runs him down.

We see Yuri letting himself into the office entrance of his brownstone. He is just in time for his appointment with Margo Goldhart. We see the therapy session in brief, Yuri dozing during one of the patient's monologues. You don't think I'm attractive, do you? she says. He asks her if there's some way he can prove to her he finds her attractive. When Margo leaves, Yuri falls asleep in his chair. Adrienne comes in and stands by the door, waiting for him to notice her.

I'm a bit vague this morning, he says. Is it your turn to use the office? She shakes her head. We should have separate offices, he says.

Adrienne sits down in the patient's chair, facing Yuri. What are your plans? she asks.

We cut to the front of the building where we see Carroway studying the entrance, undecided as to what to do. When we cut back to Adrienne and Yuri, she is sitting on his lap.

This doesn't mean I forgive you, she says. It represents a failure of imagination on my part. I can't imagine the rest of my life without you around. When she kisses him the chair goes over backwards. At that moment, Carroway comes in the door, a look of outrage on his face.

So this is how you behave when I'm not around to watch you, he says.

This man's my husband, says Adrienne.

Don't make a fool out of me, he says. It's a mistake to make an enemy out of me.

Go away, Carroway, says Yuri.

I won't forget this, Carroway says. I'm the figure hiding in the closet in your worst dreams. We see him leave and get into his red sports car which is double-parked in front of the house. We cut back to Yuri and Adrienne sitting on the floor, back to back. They are laughing so hard tears come to their eyes.

It is the next day. We see Yuri parking his car around the corner from his house. He gets out—he has his suitcase in hand—is whistling to himself. Going up the steps, he has a premonition and turns abruptly as if he expected someone to be coming up behind him.

Yuri double locks the door when he gets inside the house, calls to Adrienne. He gets no answer and calls her name again. He calls his daughter's name.

He goes through his mail, checks for messages, then takes his suitcase up to the bedroom, somewhat surprised to find the door shut. He hesitates, listens at the door for sounds, before throwing the door open.

This is what he sees: his wife and daughter in bed next to each other, lying motionless. At first he thinks they're asleep and he lets out a sigh of relief or pleasure (who knows what else he might have imagined). He smiles at the spectacle. When he gets closer he sees that there is blood on the cover of the bed, that they have been shot, that they are both dead.

Yuri is too shocked to respond. There is a hiatus of perhaps a second between his mouth opening and the scream that breaks loose. The camera freezes at this moment of his grief and horror, the scream fading then returning from a distance like an echo. When the camera releases Yuri he collapses against the wall. There is no sound, though Yuri continues to scream.

The End.

(Alternative Ending)

Adrienne is kissing Yuri when Carroway comes in the door, a look of outrage on his face.

So this is how you behave when I'm not around to watch you, he says to Adrienne.

This man's my husband, she says.

It doesn't matter. I take everything as a personal betrayal. Get out of here, Carroway, says Yuri.

I'm giving notice, says Carroway. I see this as the conclusion of my therapy. We see him leave and get into his red sports car, which is double-parked in front of the house. Anna Marie is waiting for him in the passenger seat.

It is the next day. We see Yuri emerging from his car, suitcase in hand. Going up the steps of his house, whistling to himself, he has a premonition and turns abruptly as if he expected someone to be coming up behind him. We follow his glance to a red sports car that resembles Carroway's; the car is parked across the street (in a No Parking zone) and toward the far corner. Yuri double locks the door when he gets inside, calls to his wife and daughter.

Yuri checks the therapy schedule on the bulletin board and discovers that Adrienne is downstairs with a patient. She has left a note for him.

Yuri,
Rebecca is at Dora's house. We need coffee.
Love you.

A.

Yuri carries his suitcase up to the bedroom and is surprised to find the door shut. He hesitates before opening the door, then thrusts it open. What he sees is this: in his marital bed, Carroway and Anna Marie are in the throes of the sexual act. Yuri watches in fascination, unable to avert his eyes. Carroway and Anna Marie. Anna Marie and Carroway. The image freezes.

Ten

Marital Therapy: Pro & Con

A

The phone is ringing. I am not in. (Adrienne is busy giving birth to herself.) I let the answering device represent me in my absence.

The call is from Carroway. It is the third this month. (I have an instinct for avoiding him.) I get up with excessive care and go to the bathroom for a valium. I feel invaded. I put the valium on my tongue. It slips out of my mouth before I can fill the cup with water.

A brief meeting with Carroway yesterday. He was seductive and childish. This man has nothing for me, I told myself. His presence is a kind of compelling absence. One needs to fill the space he has left vacated. That is his attraction. He is a living black hole. He is beautiful (like some poisonous flower) and he is not really there. Therefore he is dangerous. Such knowledge as I had was no real protection from him. I went with him on empty pretext (we had met for drinks at a noisy bar, could not hear ourselves talk) to his studio, which was four blocks away. I went to his studio to look at his latest painting. That was another pretext. He needed to have my critique. The painting required my acknowledgement to exist. In his space, he had me. He asked (as if he needed to ask), if I wanted to go to bed. I said absolutely not It was a straight-faced lie. We shook hands instead. It was not prelude to the main event. It was the event itself. I went home empty.

After the valium works its witchery, I do a drawing of a nude male figure (of no one real, though it bears some resemblance to Carroway) with a penis that looks like an antler. I rip out the page from my book and file it under A (for antler or aberration). Or ambivalence. Or Adrienne.

Is it the message of the drawing that penises are really weapons? Perhaps the disfigured penis points the other way. It demystifies the weapon.

(Why didn't Thomas call back? Why isn't this more than friend concerned about my reasons for calling off our date? Since we've become lovers, we seem to be running on different tracks.)

Alone in the house, listening to "The Marriage of Figaro" on QXR, I start to giggle to myself. The image of the penis- antler gets to me. I try to keep a serious face and keep breaking up. What a funny drawing that is! What a funny thing to do!

I make myself a cup of Camomille Tea and treat myself to a Cadbury bar I had been hiding in my purse. I had been saving it as a reward for the appropriate moment. This is my treat to myself. I take tiny bites. The chocolate nourishes me. It is like love. It is the very thing.

My mind does a walkabout (there's something I'm supposed to remember) during my single morning session. I have a way of listening to things, hearing them with my feelings without focusing on words. My patient, Kermit Epstein, had been obsessing for months about his wife being a kind of vampire. I understood the feeling, had similar soundings myself in connection with Yuri. I understood the feeling, but not the real issue the feeling disguised. As Kermit is pursuing his obsession (and my mind is elsewhere), I am struck with an insight. Kermit is afraid of his wife (has invested his wife with frightening powers) because he is greatly dependent on her—more so than he knows and much more so than he is able to admit. The vampire business is a protective disguise. If she leaves him, he has the feeling that his life would leave with her. It would be like having his blood drained, or (the emotional equivalent) being denied suck—having the breast taken away. He is absolutely terrified, this grown man, of being weaned. No wonder he resents the woman and is unable to stand up to her. "Why don't I leave her?" he asks himself in different words again and again. And I don't have the answer (not the real answer) until I am removed from his monologue by distraction. "Because you're afraid you'll die without her." The answer repeats itself. Echoes for me.

What I had forgotten is that today is the day I am supposed to go with Yuri to this family therapist to discuss (as if everything hadn't already been laid bare) the disrepair of our marriage. I dread the prospect.

Y

I harbor the illusion that my life is in the process of radical change. The illusion is based on a few uncharacteristic gestures, only one of which comes to mind. I took off from the hospital yesterday morning, went to Barney's and bought myself a pair of hundred and fifty dollar shoes marked down to a hundred and nine ninety five. I wore them away from the store, my feet embraced by their luxurious leather, until the right one began to pinch at the small toe. I took them off during lunch with Peter, lined them up under the table like an extra set of feet. I grieved at their betrayal, thought of returning them, though there was no time for that. There was barely time to hear the conclusion of Peter's story, which concerned a new woman in his life.

There was a revised self in my mirror, an adventurous misery in the eyes. I no longer concerned myself with Adrienne's moods, accepted the rift between us as an illness not susceptible to treatment. On the drive over to Peter and Barbara's annual party, she rested her hand on my arm. "Let's not stay late," she said. "Okay?"

What did it mean, I thought, her saying she didn't want to stay late? I found myself analyzing her remark—the more innocuous the more puzzling—as if it were one of the more significant riddles of the Sphinx.

The party was as it always was, some fifty people milling about in two large rooms, the buzz of conversation like some industrial noise. I returned Peter's obligatory bear hug, pushed my way to the bar, had a Scotch and water, ordered a refill, and only then looked over the room. I saw Adrienne, smiling brilliantly, flitting among the crowd, a wilting butterfly. I knew about half the people there, all therapists of one denomination or another. I was too sober to face them without another drink.

Barbara came over, appeared from nowhere, and asked, with exaggerated concern, how I was getting along.

The question had no context for me. "Terrific," I said.

"You look wasted, you know?" she said. "Peter and I are worried about you."

I had known Barbara for fifteen years and I had never before—perhaps once or twice in a small way—been excited by her presence. When she touched my hand, I felt the heat rush to my face. "You're looking very fetching tonight," I said. "Your hair is different."

"I had a cut," she said. "Peter thinks it's too short. Do you like it?"

"I think it looks sexy," I said. "You look a little like what's her name, the actress who's been rediscovered. Louise Brooks."

Blushing, Barbara averted her face. "Yuri, that's very

nice," she said, "even if I don't know who Louise Brooks is. ... I want to show you something. All right?"

I followed her, carrying my fourth or fifth Scotch, into the master bedroom—the bed piled halfway to the ceiling with coats. There was another person in the room, a man standing at the window smoking a cigarette.

"I fell in love with it at sight," Barbara said, pointing out a painting on the wall, a somber turn-of-the-century landscape in shadings of dark brown and black. "Peter thinks it's too dark. I want a second opinion from you."

It was nearly impenetrable in the half light. "It's like glimpsing the secret world through veils of mist," I said.

"I like that," she said. "Secret veils of mist. Yes."

When the man with the cigarette wandered out, I put my arm around Barbara's waist and kissed her. The gesture seemed to make itself, was without premeditation.

When we came apart Barbara turned toward the door to see if anyone had seen us. We moved against the wall alongside the door and kissed again, mouths open, bodies contending for the same space. It was like passion, had the form of. We separated when someone knocked at the closed door. A woman I didn't know came into the room, nodded at me, made her way to the pile of coats. "I'm glad you liked the picture," Barbara said.

It was like an enchantment. For twenty minutes I had been in love with Barbara. When I reentered the party it was over.

I caught a glimpse of Adrienne's face in a moment of repose— the willed animation gone—and I could see how sad she was. It was sad to see her sad. It struck me that she knew I had kissed Barbara. I started over to comfort her— it wasn't my job anymore—but I never got there. She was talking to Peter.

I have almost no memory of what came next, though I do remember an argument I got into with a foolish man who had written a fashionable book debunking Freud. When I finished with him—a crowd gathered around us—there was a smattering of applause. After that, I made the rounds, gave myself willingly to the gameplay of the party.

At about midnight, we collected our coats and said our goodbyes. "Don't go," Peter said. "There's a story I want to tell you."

"We have to go," I said, mumbling something about getting the sitter home on time. Meanwhile, Adrienne, her coat over her shoulders like a cape, slipped into an intense conversation with the man who had written the nasty book on Freud.

Peter's story went like this. A couple we both knew, both therapists, had gone on a late night talk show whose subject was how husbands and wives in the same field deal with the inevitable competitiveness. The couple, Henry and Illana Quixote, were so pleased with themselves, with the brilliance of their arrangement, they seemed to think it a social responsibility to present their marriage on television. They had never seen the show before, did not know that the show's smarmy right wing host, Hilton Safflower, had made a jackal's career out of making public fools of people wiser and more accomplished than himself.

Out of the corner of my eye, I noticed the celebrity-therapist write something on the inside cover of a match-book and hand it to Adrienne.

After introducing his guests—there were three couples on the show—Safflower interviewed the husbands and wives outside the others' hearing. Though they are presented as serious inquiry, the questions are designed to provoke extreme responses. The wives' remarks are passed on, out of context, to the husbands and the husbands' responses, similarly distorted, back to the wives. Safflower is skillful at manipulation, evokes hostility as if it were music from an orchestra. Before the program is over, Henry and Illana have been provoked into belittling each other before a sizeable national audience. As a consequence of their performance on television, they have stopped talking, feel betrayed, have begun to talk to lawyers about division of property. That was Peter's story. I took it as a parable of my own situation.

In the elevator on the way down, I fantasized asking Adrienne if the Freud-debunker had given her his phone number. I imagined her asking in return what Barbara and I were doing in the bedroom the half hour or so we had been missing from the party.

And then. The car was not where I remembered parking it, was not even on the same street. I was abashed. Adrienne gave an impatient turn of the head, muttered something I was meant to hear and not meant to understand. She of course had no idea where the car was, had not been paying attention. It was not her responsibility, she said. We got into a brief shouting match on the street. Adrienne walked off in a huff, hailed a cab that refused to stop, then returned on the run to ask me for money for transportation. I had no time for her. All my time was invested in trying to remember where I had left the car.

It was as if I had lost myself. I had a few inspired recollections, flashes of memory that came to nothing. The car was in none of the several places I remembered leaving it. It was only after I decided to walk home—we were no more than fifteen blocks away—that the car appeared, found me before I found it. "Here it is," I said to Adrienne, but she was not next to me or behind me or anywhere to be seen. I spent the next several minutes driving up and down streets looking for Adrienne. Not finding her, I assumed she had gotten a taxi or taken a bus and I drove in slow-motion—the precaution of the semi-unconscious—home. Adrienne wasn't back (I left the car double-parked in front of the house), which presented a logistics problem. I couldn't drive the baby-sitter, Sandy, home without someone to stay with Rebecca while I was gone. Anyway, Sandy had fallen asleep on the living room couch, so I decided to wait for Adrienne's imminent return.

I dozed off in the overstuffed art deco arm chair. When I opened my eyes—only a split second seemed to have passed— Sandy was sitting up on the couch staring at me. "I didn't want to wake you," I said. "I wasn't really sleeping," she assured me. I glanced at my watch, which has no numbers, and I wasn't sure whether almost one or almost two hours had stolen away since we left the party. Sandy said with her usual combination of timidity and complaint that she really ought to get home.

I had no idea where Adrienne might be, called the Konigs and got Barbara on the phone. "I hope I didn't wake you," I said.

"Somehow I expected you to call," she said in a hushed voice.

Sandy stood behind me with her coat on, waiting with a show of restrained impatience. "Did Adrienne come back to your place after we left?" I asked.

"Adrienne?" Barbara said, as if she were trying to place the name. "Did you have a fight?"

"Well," I said. I was embarrassed in front of Sandy, who was seventeen years old and tended to romanticize us, to explain the occasion of Adrienne's absence.

"I'm a little confused," Barbara said. "I thought you were calling about something else."

"I have to take the sitter home," I said. "If she shows up there, have her call me, will you? I don't think there's anything to worry about."

I checked Rebecca's room—she was there, she was in her bed— covered her and drove Sandy home. I was panicked, drove as quickly as I could within reason, went through what seemed like an endless red light, Sandy babbling about something Rebecca had done, something mildly (unintelligibly) unacceptable.

I found a parking space two blocks from the house, locked the keys in the car in my haste, and hurried back.

I imagined Rebecca waking to find no one home, becoming hysterical, Adrienne returning—the two of them in the living room awaiting me with outrage as I came through the door.

The house was as I had left it, silent and seemingly empty, Rebecca still asleep, Adrienne still unaccounted for. I obsessed about possibilities—mugging, rape, murder, assignation with a lover—then I had a glass of port (does it matter what I drink, is it part of the story?), and went up to bed.

I had a shock when I came into the dark bedroom, a nasty scare. Someone was lying curled up on my side of the bed. I thought—this was the way my thinking went—Sandy had had a boyfriend over and they had made out and he had fallen asleep in my bed. I was about to wake him when I realized it was not a man but a woman, that it was Adrienne and that she had been upstairs all the time. The feelings of relief exhausted me. I took off my shoes, lay down on her side of the bed, and went to sleep.

A

Yuri and I pick Rebecca up from school together and take her, my sweet baby, to Yuri's mother's apartment. (For some reason, Sandy, Rebecca's usual sitter was not available, though I don't remember why.) I see this visit as another example of not being able to say no to Yuri.

"Is this something you feel we have to do?" I ask him in the taxi on the way over.

"Come on. Adrienne. You suggested the idea."

"Really, why should I suggest such a thing. Does this seem to you something I would want to do?"

"This is crazy, Adrienne."

(That you want me to think myself crazy is something unforgivable.)

The therapist, Helena Wimpole, a scatty woman of about sixty- five with short limp white hair that seems conspicuously uncombed (her statement about herself), meets us in the cluttered living room of her East Side apartment. She has a reputation, according to Yuri's analyst, of being particularly deft with couples.

I find her, I must confess, unsympathetic on sight.

I sit down on the blue and orange flowerprint sofa and Yuri occupies a forties pale green empire chair on the other side of the room.

"I've never met with married therapists before," she says. "I must say I'm a little nervous."

We both smile on cue, trying to outdo one another at being the good child. I feel a wave of hysteria, then it passes, and I think: I have nothing to to worry about from this woman.

She explains procedure, which she calls "ground rules." Every other sentence moves into digression. Each of us (apparently) is to spell out her (or his) sense of what's gone wrong with our marriage. After that (I'm not sure of the sequence, have difficulty listening to her), we will have opportunity to respond to what's been said.

"Who wants to be first, folks?" she asks, looking at Yuri.

"Adrienne can start," he says.

"I think I'd prefer to go second," I say, conscious of looking Mrs. Wimpole directly in the eye. "It was Yuri's idea to have this joint session. I was the more reluctant one."

"Yes?" Dr. Wimpole asks as if my remark had surprised her. "When I was younger, I always hated to be the one to speak first. Now the more opportunity I have to talk, the better I like it."

I glance over at Yuri to see if he finds this woman as

absurd as I do. He refuses to meet my glance. This is a competition for him.

"It's all right," he says. "I'll start. (Is it his anxiety or mine that I feel? I avert my eyes.) "About nine months ago, I became aware that Adrienne was turning away from me."

"It was longer ago than that," I say.

"You'll have your turn," Dr. Wimpole says in a mildly reproachful voice. "Please don't interrupt your husband."

Yuri offers Dr. Wimpole his most loveable smile. She seems to melt in its glow. I sense an alliance forming between them. Is Yuri the brilliant and loving son she never had and has fantasized for herself? (Is that it, Yuri?)

I can't listen to him. It is painful to me to listen. He is so full (fool) of words. "We had been especially close," I hear him saying, "and I found her repeated rejections painful and incomprehensible. When I confronted her about it, she said she was going through something and needed more time to herself. I could understand that. I backed off, I gave her the space she asked, but it only seemed to embitter her more. Blah blah blah blah blah blah blah. But she made it increasingly clear that she didn't want blah blah with me, neither blah, nor blah, nor even—I say this with difficulty—blah."

"Did she give any reason for it?" Dr. Wimpole asks, a cunning look on her face. "If something like that were happening to me, I would ask for reasons."

This is what I am thinking. (These two are in this together. They are both, Yuri and Wimpole, versions of my mother.) What must Helena think of me? What a bad wife, this Adrienne is! She does not treat this man, her husband, with the proper respect.

I half-expect that she will send me to my room after Yuri finishes his story.

Yuri is having his turn. I try to listen. "One time," he is saying, "she thought we had been too dependent on one another and that blah blah blah blah. Another time she said she was no longer yatatta yattata yattata." He looks toward me and I wink at him. "Yeah," he says, "also that she had sole responsibility for taking care of the house and for the bringing up of Rebecca, neither of which has truth. I'm here because I want to work things out."

I clap politely at his conclusion. Good show, Yuri!
"And what do you want?" Dr. Wimpole asks me.
What do I want? "To tell you the truth," I say, "I don't really want to be here." My voice is unhesitating, calm. (This is a sincere person, the observer will think.) "I don't know what Yuri's talking about. It's been a long time since we've been close. I would say more like two years than nine months. I think it's significant that he didn't notice that I wasn't responding to him in the same way."

"What makes you so sure I didn't notice?" he says, interrupting me.

"You've had your say," I say, looking pointedly at Dr. Wimpole. "It's my turn now. Do you want to hear what I have to say, or do you want to speak both parts?"

She shakes her finger at Yuri, a flirtatious reproach. "You have my word that Yuri won't interrupt again," she says.

"It's interesting that you felt the need to speak for him," I say. I laugh good-naturedly.

"I was speaking for myself," says this paragon. "Please go on, Arianne."

"It's interesting," I continue, "because women tend to be protective of him. Women fall over themselves to take care of the poor man. That's his appeal; that's the appeal he makes to ...."

This time Dr. Wimpole interrupts. "Are you saying, Arianne, that you believe your husband is having something with another woman?"

"That's not what I'm saying," I say. "What I'm saying is (for a moment my mind is blank), that Yuri has a way of getting his way without you knowing that it's happening. That's one of my reasons, but I don't do things for reasons.

I really thought we had this good marriage. I thought, you know, that Yuri was this perfect man. Yuri is wonderful and I am this crazy dissatisfied bitch. I have this wonderful husband. I have this satisfying career. Why aren't I overwhelmingly happy? I must be this terrible person. Then I got involved with this man and I saw, you know, there were things about myself, needs really, I had never given attention to. I kept asking myself, Why are you doing this, Adrienne? I slowly began to realize that there was something wrong with my marriage to Yuri. I was changing and Yuri was not. I came to see that Yuri was incapable of change." (Wimpole looks taken aback, rushes her hand through her hair.) "I'm afraid I'm not articulate," I add.

Yuri is saying something. "Why didn't you come to me and tell me you were unhappy?" he says in a booming voice.

"Well, why didn't you notice I was unhappy," I say. "Why did it never cross your mind? You know why—it's because you don't see things."

"I didn't know our marriage was supposed to be a test," he shouts at me. "I failed your test, Adrienne, because you wanted me to fail."

"I knew that was coming," I say, my voice rising. "Speaking of self-fulfilling behavior. Look, I don't need you to analyze me. You think you're the only one who knows anything. You don't know anything I don't know."

He turns to Dr. Wimpole as if to say, Look what I have to put up with. See how unreasonable this woman is.

"I think we've reached a counter-productive point, people," Dr. Wimpole says. "Back up for a moment if you will. I'd like to give you my observations regarding what I've heard so far. All right? Do you people think you can listen to what I say without interrupting or shouting at each other?"

"That's why we're here," I say.

Yuri looks unhappy, says nothing.

With a kind of ritual fussiness, as if her hands had not told the rest of her what they were doing, Dr. Wimpole locates a pair of glasses on an end table and puts them on, raising them to her forehead after a single glance at each of us. "First of all," she says, "I'm not at all sure why you're here. I'm speaking of the woman primarily, but I'm not excluding the man. Let's put that on the table, people. This man says he wants his wife, but she doesn't want anything to do with him and he's angry as blazes at her for pushing him away. This woman is also angry. She says she thought she was happy married to this man, but it wasn't true and so she has gone elsewhere to find Mr. Happiness. Has it been established whether happiness was found elsewhere?"

"It's not as simple as that," I say. "Yes, she did. But it's not working out."

"As I've said, I'm not in the least bit sure why you've come to see me," she says, giving me what I take to be a censorious glance. Let me establish that fact before moving on to the next fact. I like to move slowly. Would you believe it, people? As I get older, I feel no urgency to move on to the next place. Well, here you are. I don't know what to say to you people. You're both too old for me to take over my knee and spank."

She closes her eyes. "Uh huh," she says to herself, acknowledging some private revelation. "Uh huh. Uh huh. My sister was in a marriage like yours for years and it drove her what I call bananas. She was always halfway bananas, but that's my sister Hortense for you. No two situations are exactly the same. My sister Hortense is not the best example. She died of a kidney infection before she ever found the time to get divorced. I think the world would have come to a halt before Hortense ever got around to filing the necessary papers." She opens her eyes and seems surprised to find us in the room with her. "You have a child, is that right? You have a child of twelve if I remember, which is a problematic age."

"She's ten actually," I say, mumbling apologetically as if her failure to be twelve were my fault.

"Her name is Rebecca," Yuri says, seems to say. (I don't

seem able to pick up what he says.)

"I didn't hear that," Dr. Wimpole says. "I have some hearing loss in my left ear. It's something that happened when I was a girl. I was the most reckless and impetuous little girl. It surprises me I ever grew up."

"Her name is Rebecca," we both say, almost in one voice.

"How is this child, Rebecca, getting along?" Dr. Wimpole asks Yuri.

"She's very lovely," I say. "Is that something one shouldn't say about one's own child." I listen to myself laugh.

"Children know so much of what's going on even if you're very careful in front of them," Dr. Wimpole says in her scatty way. "I could tell you some stories about my niece Bernadette, but I don't think we have time for that today."

"Rebecca has bad dreams," Yuri says. "She has trouble sleeping through the night."

"Yuri tends to exaggerate," I say, shaking my head at him. "It's happened at most three times in the past several months."

"It's more like three times a week," Yuri says. "Adrienne doesn't want to believe her behavior has any impact on her child's life."

"Come off it," I say. "And how would you know how often Rebecca wakes up at night? You're always asleep when she comes in our room. I'm the one who has to deal with it."

"Last Wednesday," Yuri says, "when Rebecca woke from a bad dream I stayed with her in her room until it was morning."

"Big deal," I say.

"You both want to get credit for what you've been doing," Dr. Wimpole says. "You feel, both of you people, that you don't get enough credit from the other. Yes?"

I am readily credulous. Even banalities tend to surprise me with their disguised old news. "Is that really true?" I ask

143

Yuri, who has his hands clasped in his lap and is staring morosely at the ceiling.

Yuri takes refuge in looking the other way. He can't admit he wants anything from me, which is sad. (Is it not?) I see him for the moment with absolute clarity. Dr. Wimpole is leaning forward, head tilted, listening with her good ear to the unspoken.

Y

Adrienne was looking into the office, was self-absorbed, when I came up behind her. When I touched her shoulder to let her know I was there she let out a gasp. "Where did you come from?" she cried. She had her hand on her heart as if reciting The Pledge of Allegiance. A vein stood out on her forehead. She squeezed by me in the doorway, some contact between us unavoidable. Her elbow thumped my chest. I had a hard-on, which grazed her hip. She had a faint, knowing smile on her face, a child's leer.

I forced her against me for a second or so, then let her go. "I have a patient coming any minute," I said.

"I wouldn't be surprised," she said. She moved up the stairs with a kind of insect intensity. I watched her go away. A moment later, she called to me from the top of the steps. "Yuri, if you want to phone Dr. Wimpole, it's all right with me."

I was all over the place, walked back and forth, stared at myself in the full length office mirror. An imposter stared back at me. My clothes hung on me. My face looked raw-edged and incomplete as if it had been torn from its mold. Fucking Adrienne, I felt, was the only thing that could heal me.

When my patient arrived, I was all right, felt magically in control. He was boy of twelve named Alex, a wise child, who had come to me with irrational fears of abandonment. I had been seeing him now for four months and we had made some small progress. He had agreed to sleep over a friend's house the past weekend and he was coming today to report to me about the experience.

It is dangerous for a therapist to be dependent for satisfaction on his patients' breakthroughs.

Alex had cancelled the sleepover, was aggrieved with himself. We reviewed the events immediately preceding his change of heart. His mother had visited him in his room, had urged him to go to the party in a way that fueled his anxiety. They had a fight about something and she left his room, saying she was very unhappy with him. He lay in bed for a while, masturbating. When he heard her coming upstairs, he buried himself in his covers. She said he better get ready if he was going to the party and he shouted back that he wasn't going. Until he announced he wasn't going, he hadn't actually decided. She asked him if he was afraid to go and he said yes and she sat down next to him like someone in a sickroom—Alex's image—and hugged him.

I saw an insight flash across his face. When I asked him what it was, he shook his head in denial.

It was after the session was over, when he had already gotten up from his chair, that he said, "She was afraid of my leaving her."

I nodded. We shook hands. I felt hopeful at that moment for both of us.

This was the next day. After clinic, I went for a drink with Peter, listened to his confession, shared complaints about our wives, went back with him to his apartment. He didn't want to be alone with Barbara and I didn't want to go home to Adrienne.

I sat between them on the sofa, drinking champagne, fussed over and admired. At some point, Barbara invited me to stay for dinner.

I said—it was an automatic response—that I had to call home to see if Adrienne had anything special planned.

"Don't call," Peter said.

I dialed my number, got a busy signal, returned to my place between them on the couch.

"I take full responsibility for your not calling home," Peter said. "Let her worry about you."

"That's stupid, Peter," Barbara said. There was a knife edge of anger in her voice. "If Yuri feels he has to call, it's not your business to object. He's the kind of man who doesn't want his family to worry about him."

"That's an ignorant remark," Peter said. "The man has got to show his wife he's unpredictable."

I got Rebecca on the phone. We talked for a few minutes, made small talk as if I hadn't seen her for weeks. "Last night, I woke up in the middle of the night and couldn't get to sleep," she said.

"I know, honey," I said. "I was there. What are you and Mom doing about dinner?"

Momentarily, Adrienne was at my ear. "Hi," she said.

"Adrienne, I'm at Peter and Barbara's," I said

"Are you?" she said. "How nice."

"They've asked me to stay for dinner," I said. "You don't mind, do you?"

"Why should I mind?" she said in her extraterrestrial voice. "Really. Why should you think I would mind?"

"Well, I just wanted to let you know where I am."

"And you have," she said. "We'll see you later, I suppose." She hung up.

"He was wrong, wasn't he?" Barbara said when I returned to my place between them on the couch.

"Look at the man's face, Babs," Peter said. "That face

has just made contact with a closed door."

The meal, which featured a roast of some sort, made almost no impression. I ate little, tasted nothing. Peter and Barbara were a model of decorum, a seminar in domestic diplomacy. I was aware of having had too much to drink and not enough to eat. Although barely able to stand up, I announced that it was time for me to go.

Barbara said, "You can stay the night, Yuri. We can find some place to put you."

"He's not going to stay," Peter said. "Don't waste your breath on him, Babs. The man has got to get home to his family."

"I appreciate this, my friends," I said. I was standing at the door with my coat on. I kissed Barbara, hugged Peter. I feel very close to you both."

Peter and Barbara embraced me from opposite sides, held me between them.

"You mean a lot to us," Peter said.

"We love you," said Barbara, hugging me.

The room behind them, the extended hallway, seemed filtered through yellow smoke.

"I am very moved," I said or thought of saying.

"We want you to know," Peter said, "that if you need a place to stay, there's always a bed for you in our house."

Barbara kissed me on the side of the mouth, said, "If I weren't married to Peter, you would be the man I would want to be with."

Tears came to my eyes. "Thank you, friends," I said. "I love you both."

Peter leaves with me, Barbara stands in the doorway waving.

Peter and I walk several blocks in various directions, looking for my car. It is the second time in two weeks, both during visits to the Konigs, that it has disappeared.

The house is mostly dark when I let myself in. I am elated at having found my car, at having found a parking place for it, at having arrived home safely, feel oddly— tremulously—triumphant. Rebecca loves me. I look into Rebecca's room, discover her bed has not been slept in. I look into my own bedroom, find neither wife nor daughter. The emptiness of the house confuses me.

Eventually I discover that Adrienne has left me a note wedged into the kitchen phone like a flower.

> Yuri—
> I'm having a drink with a friend. Rebecca is sleeping at Olivia's house. Don't wait up for me.

I flop down on the couch, turn on the television with the remote, watch sports and weather—I suffer Rebecca's absence, the empty house—the weather map dissolving into an old movie. I doze, wake, fight off sleep. I see snatches of a black and white movie, a detective story with the ambience of a bad dream. A man is pushed out of a skyscraper window, screams as he falls, his mouth agape like a wound. The detective is questioning a woman—she puts her arms around his neck. I think to warn him that she can't be trusted. He kisses her. The door behind him opens. Adrienne, looking like she has fallen from a window, comes into the room.

She calls my name, moves to the television to turn it off.

Half-asleep, I rise from the sofa like an apparition. What do you think you're doing?" I say. "The murder is still unsolved."

She gasps, says, "God, you scared me half to death."

A

Dr. Wimpole is wearing her mischievous look. "Have I said something I wasn't supposed to say," she says. "Tell you the truth, people, I'm not in the least bit sorry."

I don't know what she's talking about. I look at Yuri, who seems equally befuddled. "I don't think parenting is an issue where Adrienne and I are at odds," he says.

"I think Yuri's been mostly a good father," I say.

"I didn't know you thought I did anything well," Yuri says.

That's a sad thing for him to say. "You're not such a bad father," I say to him.

"Thank you," he says with what I take to be irony.

Wimpole has a secret smile on her face. "What do you think of Adrienne as a mother?" she asks Yuri.

He doesn't answer right away, which is a message in itself. "I never said Adrienne wasn't a good mother," he says in a dead voice.

"Why don't you tell that to her?" Wimpole says.

I want to cry when she says that. I have this image of myself as a child standing in front of a class, getting ready to recite some lesson I failed to prepare. Getting it wrong was unthinkable. It was my role to be perfect.

This scatty woman we have turned ourselves over to asks me what my reaction is to what Yuri has said.

"What did Yuri say? I'm sorry. I didn't realize he said anything."

"It may be the case, let me put it to you, that you preferred not to hear him," Wimpole says. "Could that be possible, Arianne?"

"I think that's probably true," I say.

"I said I felt you were a good mother," he says. He refuses to look at me.

"Did you?" I look over at Wimpole. I assume the issue

is concluded. "We don't always see eye to eye on what's best for Rebecca," I hear myself say.

"How did you feel, Arianne, when Yuri said you were a good mother?" Wimpole asks me. "Were you in touch with your feelings?"

I resist her manipulation. "Of course I like to be praised," I say. "Who doesn't like to be praised? I would have liked it better if it were less grudging. I felt he was saying it mostly for your benefit."

"Why for my benefit, of all things?" she says.

"He wants you to like him," I say. "He wants you to see him as the good person in this marriage."

Her feathery white hair floats about in all directions when she nods. "Oh I don't matter," she says. "Yuri knows that." She gives a girlish shrug. "If Yuri's the good person, Arianne, does that make you the bad person? The secretly no-one-knows- how-good-I-am bad person."

"That's a bit easy, isn't it?" I say.

"I have no illusions," Wimpole says. "There's nothing under the sun that I can tell you that you don't already know in spades. Arianne, how would you have responded if you felt your husband's compliment were genuine?"

"I don't understand what you're asking," I say. "By the way, my name is pronounced Adrienne. I don't anticipate my feelings, Dr. Wimpole. I can only know what they are when I experience them."

"Arianne, in my opinion as observer," Wimpole says, "Yuri was being sincere."

I look over at Yuri who has his usual severe countenance. "Did you mean it?" I ask him.

"I meant it," he says. He adds my name to the sentence as an afterthought.

I turn away, turn my face away. I feel ashamed. "I don't know that I really believe him," I say. "I don't know that. And even if he meant it, I don't see that it changes anything."

Yuri rests his head on his hand.

"It sounds to me as if Arianne...Adrienne is rejecting you," Wimpole says to him. "How does that make you feel?"

"I don't know," he says from behind his hand. "I have trouble believing she means it."

My voice is like ice against glass. "Yuri tends to ignore what he doesn't want to hear," I hear myself saying. "He has a talent for obliviousness."

"Fuck off," he says.

"He also tends to be insulting," I say.

"What I hear," Wimpole says, "is that you don't want to give this man anything. And this man may want everything, but he doesn't know how to ask. Is that accurate? Is that an observation to be put on the table, people?" Her glasses slide down her forehead and she removes them in annoyance.

"She wants to kill me," Yuri says, "and she wants me to look after her after I'm dead."

"Shhhh," Wimpole says. She puts her finger across her lips and holds it there.

I close my eyes, try to listen to my feelings, but hear only static. "I feel that I don't want to give myself to Yuri ever again," I hear myself saying. "I'm willing to fix his meals, but I don't want to give anything of myself to him. I don't want to be touched by him ever again." It is as if there is a loudspeaker right behind my head that reproduces these words. Yuri lets out a groan from his side of the room and I don't dare to look at him. I feel in my jacket pocket for a kleenex and find some ancient wadded piece which I use to blot my eyes. "I feel I'm terrible," I say.

Wimpole gives me this motherly smile. "That's clear," she says in her no nonsense manner. "You don't want to have any intimacy with this man."

I nod, though I sense she is representing me in some willfully dense way. (Is she making fun of me? Mocking me?)

I am aware of how I look to the others, how ugly, eyes red, eyeliner running. Yuri hands me a box of kleenex and I blow my nose. I hold the box on my lap like a child. "He really has no idea of who I am," I say. "He thinks of me as some virgin...version of himself."

"That's bullshit," he shouts, which makes me laugh through my tears. "I know you as well as I know myself."

"I'm never going back to you," I shout at him.

His face cracks down the middle. "I can survive without you," he mutters.

"Wait just a minute here," Wimpole says. "Yuri, do you or do you not want this woman back. I thought that was a fact we had on the table."

He sighs, this Yuri. "I don't want her this way," he says. "This isn't the woman I want."

"This is the way I am," I throw back at him. "If you can't accept that, I don't want you around."

"What I see," Wimpole says, "is a very angry woman. What is it, Arianne? What has this man done to make you so angry?"

"Adrienne's this angry lady," I say. "It's Adrienne, okay? not Arianne. I'm angry at Yuri because he doesn't really care what I do. I feel I've been deceived by him."

"You feel Yuri deceives you," she says, looking about for a figurative table to place this "fact" on. "Let me get this straight. Yuri deceives you by pretending to care for you when, in fact, he really doesn't."

"I don't think I made myself clear," I say.

"You're clear, Adrienne," she says. "You're a well spoken person, which is something I admire. If you'll bear with me, I'd like to make a statement of intent. The reason I spend my afternoons doing this, working with people like you people, is that marriage is too important, in my opinion, to leave, when in crisis, solely to the principals involved. When you marry someone, you are electing to spend the rest of your life with that person. That can be difficult. When things go haywire, you just want to run away from it as fast and as far as you can go." She seems to have lost her train of thought, makes a gesture to no point. "I'm here, people, to help you find your way back to where you were in the happy times."

I notice from the digital clock on the bookcase behind Yuri's head that there are four minutes left to our session. (What a disaster it's been.) Wimpole is asking me something. I force myself to pay attention.

"Arianne, let's forget about this man, Yuri," she is saying. "Let's put old Yuri in the closet." She mimes locking someone in the closet, which makes me smile. "Now Arianne... Adrienne, if you were getting together with another man, what would you want from this relationship?"

There is just a minute left to our fifty minute session, I note with some relief. "I really haven't given it a lot of thought," I say. "All I feel clear about is what I don't want. I don't want what I've had. Yuri refuses to accept that as a fact that's on the table."

"Yuri's in the closet," Wimpole says. "Adrienne, what do you want from this new man?"

I want to tell her that our time, which she may not have noticed, has run out. I envision another distraught couple in the waiting room, waiting to put their marriage on Wimpole's imaginary table. "What do I want?" I ask rhetorically, conscious of stalling. "First of all, I want to be treated as an equal." I indicate with a shrug that that is all I can think of under the pressure of the moment. "Yes, and I want to be treated with appropriate respect."

"I see, yes," Wimpole says, retrieving her glasses from the table, holding them in front of her eyes. She studies my face. "Is that what you want most from a man, Adrienne, respect?"

"I want him to be generous with money." I laugh. (It is meant as a joke.) "I want someone who's kind. Kindness is a high priority." Wimpole nods. "I want to be loved of course. I think that goes, doesn't it, without...." My voice breaks. Tears leak from my eyes. I am trembling. I have the sense I am so awful that no one could possibly love me. No one at all. These feelings anger me.

"Are you aware, Adrienne, that Yuri said something to you?" she asks me.

(What?) If I had strength in my legs, I would get up from the couch and leave the room. "I want kindness," I hear myself say. (I have no idea what's going on.) Yuri says something, which makes no sense. "Are you taking back what you just said?" Wimpole asks him. "That was a minute ago," he says. "My feelings have changed. If she wanted to hear what I said, she would have heard it." "What don't I want to hear," I say. I am still sobbing. "You're a narcissist, Adrienne," he says. "Your emotional age is sixteen years old going on nine. You've treated me in the last year like some derelict relative who's overstayed his welcome. You're a pain in the ass." "Why do you stay with me?" I say under my breath. "If I'm so terrible, why don't you just leave." He turns his face away. "I said I loved you," he says as though he were reading someone else's line. He won't look at me. Not enough, I tell myself. He is unable to say it with real feeling. I get up from the couch (though don't remember getting up), go over to where he sits with his eyes averted. I squeeze his hand. He looks startled. "I love you too," I hear myself say, meaning it and not meaning it. He pulls me roughly on to his lap and strokes my hair. My name is whispered to me. I rub my wet face against his. When I stop crying, I return to my place on the couch. I am out of focus. "This is probably as good a place to stop as any," Wimpole says in her bemused way. I go into the bathroom to wash my face. I go to the bathroom to get away from the others and study my face in the mirror. Yuri and Wimpole are buzzing about something outside my closed door. There is laughter. Who is laughing?

(Are you amusing her, Yuri?) As I return to the livingroom, I witness Yuri passing a check to her. She takes it with embarrassed acknowledgement as though it were a bribe. Yuri holds my coat for me. When we step out into the hall and close the door (it is a relief that Wimpole does not come home with us), he puts his arm around my waist. He pulls me to him. I feel affection for this man, though I don't know why. I let him kiss me. "I don't know what happened in there," I say. "Don't make too much of it. All right?" He walks off ahead of me without a word and presses the elevator button. As we get out of the elevator, he says, "I won't make anything of it." What a funny old lady! I want to say to him. Nothing that happened in that room can be taken seriously. Can it? I want to ask him. As if he has the answer. Therapy, it strikes me, is full of charged moments of deception.

Y

I ask Adrienne what time it is.

"Around twelve thirty," she says. The wall clock in the kitchen shows twenty minutes after one. Adrienne takes off her coat, seems not to know what to do with it.

"Who was the friend you were having your drink with?" I ask.

"It's nothing," she says as if it were one word. "It's not important." She puts her coat on the back of a chair. It slides off on to the rug.

"If it wasn't important, why did you go? And why isn't Rebecca here?"

"Sandy wasn't available," she says. "I couldn't very well leave her here by herself, now could I? It isn't anything to concern yourself about, Yuri." She goes upstairs, hurries up the steps, to the bathroom.

For what happens next, there is only my own self-doubting recollection.

I am in the hallway when Adrienne comes out of the bathroom wearing a loosely tied silk kimono, her breasts exposed. She is carrying a diaphragm in her right hand, balancing it on her palm.

Astonished, in a kind of shock, I lean against the wall to keep from falling.

She is under the covers reading a book on esthetics when I come in, my body like a furnace. "I want you to sleep downstairs," I say in a mad calm voice.

"I have no problem with that," she says, closing her book, sliding out of bed, getting into her kimono.

I sit on the bed with my back to her, more rage in my heart than I can bear to know.

"You have no idea what I want," she says as if it were the harshest thing she might tell me. She takes her undisclosed passion downstairs. The unimaginable follows. I feel punished by her absence.

After pulling off my shoes—I don't bother to untie them— I lie down fully clothed on top of the comforter. In an instant, I capitulate to exhaustion.

I wake during the night, notice the empty space in the bed next to me, go downstairs, find Adrienne curled awkwardly on the living room couch covered by one of my overcoats. "You can return," I whisper to her. She doesn't answer. I carry her up the stairs—she is astonishingly light— and put her to bed like a child.

Eleven

Behavioral Therapy

A

In an undated entry in his journal, Yuri reports an incident (a fight really) that is significantly different from my own sense of things.

We are sleepwalkers in separate dreams.

Y

I walked Barbara home in the rain after lunch. We held hands, walked the streets like teenagers pretending to be lovers.

"I need someone to hold hands with," she said. "It's what I miss most about my marriage."

I had no recollection of Peter and Barbara ever holding hands. I said goodbye to her in the lobby of her apartment building.

She was suddenly coy, said there was something she wanted to tell me, but not now, another time. I pressed her to tell me her secret. "If I told you now," she said, "you'd have no reason to ever see me again."

Adrienne, I later learned, was having lunch with Peter while I was having lunch with Barbara.

A

(Peter, your best friend Peter, propositioned me today. It is said when the check arrives face down between us. "I have always wondered what it would be like to do the sack scene with you," he says loud enough for people at the next table to hear. "What about your girl friend?" I ask him. "I don't really know if she's into threesomes," he says. We laugh together as if it were the funniest thing.)

Y

We shared impressions that evening of our friends' emotional states. We had begun to talk again in the old manner. What do I mean exactly by the old manner? We tended to discuss our friends' behavior as if we were a medical team diagnosing some new and interesting pathology. It was a form of intimacy between us.

"Now that they're apart," she said, "they've taken on aspects of the other's personality. Have you noticed that?"

I said I hadn't, not in Barbara's case at least, though I could believe it was true.

Adrienne said she worried about Barbara, that she thought it was going to be worse for her—much worse—before it got any better.

What are we talking about when we talk about Peter and Barbara?

R

This may have been in my sleep. I was going down to the basement to see my daddy in his office. I was afraid they had gone somewhere without telling me. On the steps, as I was going down, I saw this humungous bug. It wasn't moving. I touched it with the toe of my shoe to prove it wasn't dead. It made a sound like a cry and rolled boldly on to its back. It was more like a scraping sound. It scrambled back on to its front. The sound this time was like Darth Vader breathing. I ran up the stairs and closed the door behind me. I wanted to get far away from that bug and I didn't want it to know where I was going.

A

Yuri mentions a psychoanalytic conference in Zurich he has been invited to attend. I have also been invited. I have also thought of going. In postponing a decision (how difficult such trips seemed), I had forgotten about the invitation.

"You went to the last conference," I say. "Why don't you stay home with Rebecca and I'll go this time."

His face darkens as if a small bulb under the skin has gone out. "We could both go," he says. "Rebecca could stay with my mother."

I tell him he can go alone if it is important to him and I will go the next time. Do I smile? I think in this instance I do. I am thinking, This is not the rejection you are going to make of it, Yuri. This is a gesture to show you that I am not the witch you make me out to be. He says he will think about it but I can see he has no intention of going by himself. The phone interrupts us.

Peter says, "You are setting yourself up to be rejected by Yuri."

Y

Although we seem to be moving headlong in that direction, I don't want to get caught up in an affair with Barbara. We did a lot of hand holding during our exchange of confidences. And we embraced for extended moments when we said goodbye. "I think of you as the first line of my support system," Barbara said. It was the essence of what she said if not the exact words. We had the ambience of a love affair without actually making love.

I had lunch with Peter once a week and I felt, if not disloyal, somewhat compromised by my unacknowledged (unconsumated) intimacy with Barbara. At alternate times, Adrienne broke bread and exchanged confidences with Barbara or Peter, or with other mutual friends, who were separated or contemplating separation. If we had all compared notes, who knows what we might have learned. I saw little of Adrienne, tended to be downstairs when she was up, upstairs when she was down. When we talked it was to replay old conversations. I was going through the early stages of mourning. I was living with someone who, in the context of my emotional life, had recently died.

Peter took my reluctance to leave Adrienne as a personal affront. His overstated outrage had a calming effect on me, let me feel that my life was secretly better than anyone knew. For his own part, Peter professed to be overjoyed with unmarried life, though he didn't want a divorce from Barbara so he wouldn't be under pressure to marry Roberta, the twenty- nine year old pop singer he was currently dating. He was also suffering from high blood pressure and had occasional heart palpitations of non-somatic origin.

A

C's absence feeds on me like a lingering disease. I don't accept that he prefers Anna Marie. (Is prefer what it is?) I think of myself in the abstract: the nurturing woman who has been sent away.

Last week, after clinic, I went to the Moondance Diner for coffee. I sat at a table, which has an oblique view of C's loft building. Two women emerged and about five minutes later C appeared, wearing hat and dark glasses. The women came out of the building at the same time (it could have been coincidence) and went off in opposite directions. One might have been with C. My intuition was that he had been with both. That seemed less awful somehow. I watched him walk to his car, completely absorbed in himself. He looked sad. Post-coital triste? I was sad for him. I felt no jealousy, felt released from jealousy.

Y

"Face it, Yuri," Barbara said. "Adrienne is not going to go back to you." We were in her apartment, drinking espresso as black as ashes.

"How do you know this?" I asked, the question violating the implicit rules of our foursome.

Her face was flushed and she was looking away. "When Peter first moved out," she said, "what I missed most was the physical contact. I felt kind of unloveable. I was telling that to Adrienne, who was very supportive. She's a good listener. She really is. Then she said rather casually, 'Why don't you have an affair with Yuri?' I was shocked, you know, when she said it. That's what I've been wanting to tell you and couldn't."

I had no reaction, shook my head, wanted not to believe her. She moved an infinitesimal distance away. "I felt a little guilty, Yuri, as if she had caught me doing something wrong. To be frank, after you kissed me that time at the party, I had thought of it too. I felt kind of angry about it the next day. I was kind of crazed about it really."

I was thinking out loud, pursuing comprehension. "It's possible she was trying to find out if there was something between us," I said. "It may have been a way of keeping us from having an affair. Or maybe she felt she could trust me to you. According to Freud, every gesture has an almost infinite burden of meanings."

"Is she really that subtle?" Barbara asked. Our thighs were touching, and I sensed that if we were to start an affair, if it were ever going to happen, this was its moment. I had to leave, had a patient to see.

We kissed at the door several times, Barbara keeping her hands behind her back. "I'll have fantasies about you when you're gone," she said.

A

The first day I nursed coffee for over two hours. Today I had herb tea and a crumbly blueberry muffin. I was various in my behavior. A surprising person. My sketchbook was with me. I never saw C leave the building. I stayed too long, waiting for nothing. I just couldn't pull myself away. (You didn't ask where I was. I let you think what you wanted to think.)

I wrote another letter to C, the second since our break up (or is it break down?). Yuri would have said (had you known about the letters) that they were letters to myself given the displacement of a contrived occasion. I deny that of course. I was writing to a man who had loved me. If he is incapable of love (I believe and I don't believe), it is a choice C lets himself make, a kind of cowardice.

By the time I got the letter down on paper, I knew it by

heart. As soon as I folded the letter and put it in an envelope, I could barely remember a complete sentence. I wanted the letter as it was. I wanted the letter as it had been before it was a letter.

I had it photocopied (one for me and one for him) and I put the original in the addressed envelope. I carried it around in my purse for what must have been more than a week before thrusting it in the mailbox one windy Sunday morning. On two more occasions I went back to the diner. I felt at home there. The waitresses nodded to me when I came in. The one time I spotted C, he left the building in a hurry and hailed a cab. This was before I had mailed the letter. I felt lonely at being excluded from his plans.

R

There I was going down those same stairs and the same humungous bug was there waiting for me to come along. I was going to ask my mom a question when I nearly stomped on the ugly bug. I could hear my mom's voice. She was either on the phone or with a patient. B was on a different step this time. My mom was saying, "Don't expect too much from me." I pushed B with my shoe, then ran up the stairs, and escaped to my room. I hated that bug. I said this to my daddy: "Daddy, we have to call the exterminator. This house is crawling with bugs." "Is it?" he said.

Y

Melinda, who I hadn't heard from in months, was waiting for me in the anteroom of the clinic. She followed me into my office without invitation.

"How have you been?" I asked. She looked worn.

"I don't know if you want to see me," she said shyly. "I wouldn't be surprised if you didn't."

"I have a patient waiting," I said. "Could I meet you somewhere after three o'clock?"

"I just want to say that I'm all right," she said. "I'm doing all right."

"Why are you here?" I asked.

She laughed. "Well, I was talking about you in therapy and I thought it would be nice to see you again. And there you are, looking as you always look."

She was dressed all in black, tight black skirt, loose black sweater. She looked frail and sad. My attraction to her was beyond any knowledge I was prepared to share with myself. "You look very sexy," I said.

She turned her back to me and removed her raincoat, which had been open, then she unhooked her skirt and let it drop to the floor. Then crossing her arms, she lifted her sweater over her head.

Her breasts were like half-moons when she turned to face me. I kissed her open-mouthed, her fishy tongue sliding down my throat.

"There isn't time for this," I said.

She gave me a skeptical look, began in mock slow motion to get back into her sweater.

Melinda lay down on the flower-patterned linoleum floor, raised her knees. I thought of locking the door, though didn't, let the thought suffice. I was estimating how much extra time I might give my neglected patient, a timid Korean woman named Dulcie, who had been waiting for me in the other room.

"I've entered the Clinical Psychology Program at NYU," she whispered in my ear.

It was my obsession to share her obsession. "That's terrific," I said.

The sex went on longer than I had anticipated, extended itself. I imagined, as I was making love to Melinda, passive Dulcie sticking her head in the door to ask if I was ready for her.

Was this the nature of middle-aged passion? As I fucked a former patient, I was distractedly concerned with the aetiology of the one waiting to see me.

Oh Dulcie, I don't want your therapist to disillusion you, to make you doubt your own sense of appropriateness!

And then, as if conjured by my anxiety, there was a tap on the door just loud enough to assert its reality.

I didn't stop what I was doing, but said, barely turning my head, "I'll be with you in a few minutes, Dulcie."

The tapping repeated itself, became more assertive. "This is like a dream I had," Melinda said.

I shouted in outrage to whoever was there—I no longer believed it was Dulcie—"I have a patient in here with me."

The wrong remark was, as always, the truth undisguised. When we broke connection it was like waking from a week's sleep.

"You never call me," she said, aggrieved.

"You asked me not to call you," I reminded her.

She was in a sulky mood as she put on her skirt, her head turned away. "You wouldn't have called anyway."

"I'll call you and we'll get together," I said. I stroked her hair.

She turned a pout in my direction, her eyes so unutterably sad they moved me to concern. "I don't want to hear from you," she said. "I thought I could handle it, but obviously I can't."

"I want to see you again," I said.

She made a gesture with her hands that suggested pushing away. "I better go," she said. "You have this real patient waiting."

The waiting room was empty when I let Melinda out, Dulcie apparently having lost heart. I tried to separate myself from what I imagined Dulcie's feelings to be—confusion, humiliation, self-loathing—but there was no getting around that I had behaved unacceptably. I paced the small clinic room as if it were a jail cell. Then Dulcie appeared. She had been to the bathroom, she said. She had been knocking to tell me she was going to the bathroom so I wouldn't worry if I didn't see her when I opened the door.

A

After my last patient of the day, I lie down on Yuri's side of the bed and imagine Carroway receiving my letter. I try to envision his reaction as he reads (I was thinking "eats") my words. My feelings disguised as words.

As I imagine it, he refuses to open the envelope. Refuses to risk himself to the touch of my words. The prospect engenders anxiety. My words die unread.

I keep stealing looks at Yuri's journal, a new obsession. From yesterday's entry: "I can think of no greater relief than her absence from my life." I have the feeling he means me to read it. (True?) The absoluteness of the sentence upsets me. (What is the nature of this absence?) I put the journal back in its drawer without reading further. Later, I consider going back and writing a comment in the margin.

Y

I had a dream in which Barbara was offering me a part in a play she was writing called "Fire Away or Sink". My performance took place behind the curtain—in shadow— for one of those reaons that seem so compelling in dreams. I called her the next morning—dreams require an answer— from my office at the clinic. "I have the feeling we've been avoiding each other," I said. "I don't want that to be the case."

"My life is a disaster, Yuri," she said. "I need to talk to you."

So I rearranged some appointments at the clinic and went to Barbara's apartment. We didn't talk, as I assumed we would, about whether or not we would sleep together.

Barbara's subject was this: she had had a sexual encounter with a much younger man she had met at the local D'Agostino's. The man, a blue collar type, had been standing behind her in the checkout line, and they had struck up a conversation concerning a bizarre headline in "The National Enquirer." A MARTIAN FATHERED MY CHILD/ 14 YEAR OLD VIRGIN REPORTS.

The man was not her type, not someone she would have been interested in had they met through conventional channels. That was its attraction, she said. She was doing something outside the normal pattern of her behavior. He helped her with her groceries; she invited him in; one thing led to another.

"You did nothing wrong," I said, willing a distance I was unable to feel.

"You know what's crazy, Yuri"—she took my hand—"I don't even like him. Yet I'm furious, you know, that he hasn't called back. That's crazy, isn't it?"

"Well, you went to bed with him, Barbara, to make yourself feel loveable. By his not calling you, which you feel as a rejection, he's making you unlovable. You have reason to be pissed at him."

"This is very kind of you, Yuri." She squeezed my hand. "You know what? I'm in a really strange mood." She nodded to herself in corroboration and left the couch, disappearing into the kitchen. "Am I loveable? How about some coffee or a glass of wine?" She broke a glass, taking it down from the shelf, then cut her finger cleaning up. "I'm sorry," she said. Covering her face with her hands, she began to sob.

Patients cry in my office all the time, but I've never been

easy with it. I tended to take crying—women's in particular—as an unanswerable demand. "It's okay, Barbara," I said.

The crying, which had almost stopped, exploded again into violent sobs. She slumped into the nearest chair. "No one...no one loves me," she keened.

The passion of her grief frightened me. I forced myself to sit on the arm of her chair, to put my arm around her. "We all love you," I said.

She pressed her face into my chest, curled herself into me. "No one," she said fiercely. "Hold me. Okay? I'll do the same for you. Mommy."

I held her as tightly as I could, put both my arms around her, and still I felt I was failing her. "I'm here," I said.

I made love to Barbara on the floor of the living room, on her green Chinese rug.

When she returned from the bathroom—her make-up erratically restored, her lipstick like a child's drawing—she looked like a survivor of some disaster. "How can I ever look you in the face again?" she said. Her smile belied the question.

"You were fine," I said. "You were very brave."

She hugged me from behind. "You're being gallant, right? Right?"

I kissed her goodbye on the cheek, said the man from the supermarket had been a fool not to call back.

I was mildly depressed when I returned to the clinic, felt inauthentic, fraudulent.

R

What do we know about the feelings of B? That's what I was thinking right before I went to sleep. The bug said something to me in my dream. What are you trying to say, B? It was in a language I couldn't understand. It was not what you would call a human language. I got out of bed in the dark and put a blanket over my shoulders. It dragged under my feet when I walked. I looked into my Mom and Dad's bedroom. They slept with their backs to each other. Mom lifted her head and said, "Nothing in the world can make me." I walked downstairs in the dark, shining a flashlight on my feet. The floor was cold.

Y

It was not the inevitable next step, merely an acknowledgment of reality. I went to see a divorce lawyer for advice, a man named Harry Elders, who had been recommended to me as forceful from one of my colleagues at the clinic.

Elders was a youngish man—that is, he looked like a boy who had reached forty without becoming an adult—with a brash energetic manner. He radiated over-compensation. On the barest acquaintance, he announced that he fully understood my situation, that he liked to represent clients with whom he had feelings of identification. He moved between large aggressive claims—"The woman has no case—we'll destroy her pretensions"—to advising that no one can tell in advance how divorce matters will be adjudicated. His best advice was to avail myself of a first strike capacity. I told him that I wasn't ready to act, wanted merely to acquaint myself with my rights. "With due respect, doctor," he said, "from what you told me, and I've seen a number of cases like yours, divorce is the medicine I'd prescribe. The marriage, believe me, is over. Make your move before she makes it for you."

I said I would get back to him. We shook hands across his desk. His grip was forceful. He was showing me I might become more powerful by hiring him.

"You chose this man to give yourself an excuse not to act," Peter said over drinks at a new Columbus bar called *Manna from Heaven*. He was going to Roberta's place afterward for dinner and I felt—what?—a touch of envy. He seemed more than usually pleased with himself, dominated our conversation.

The streetlights had just come on, though it was not yet dark, and I was aware of being alone, of feeling an ache of loneliness. Although I knew the upper west side well, the streets remained anonymous. Wanting acknowledgment, I stared into strangers' faces, daring them to look away. I went from flashes of exhilaration to feelings of extreme vulnerability. If someone, some former patient, with an imagined grievance, wanted to assault me, there was no one to come to my aid on these streets. I felt some urgency about getting home. My anxiety focused on Rebecca and Adrienne. I needed them to need me to protect them from some kind of danger.

A woman, someone coming up from behind, called what sounded like "Yuri," not a name readily confused with something else. I stopped reluctantly.

A

In the dream, he was dancing in the street with a waitress from the diner, a blowsy gum-chewing, red-headed woman. In real life (there is that too), I am walking down the street toward the diner when I see him. He has his bow-like back curved toward me. There is a woman, who might have been the sister of the red-headed woman in the dream, holding on to his arm. They go into the building, C leading the way like a tour guide. It is so much like the dream I will myself to wake. I find myself in a phone booth and dial his number incorrectly. One digit isn't right, is blocked out. (Does it mean I don't want to make connection?) I get a busy signal and dial again. This time I know I have the right number. I anticipate his voice. My heart is buzzing. The dream, I think (the trauma), must play itself out. The phone rings twenty-one times. Someone picks up the phone and hangs it up without a word. At least he's not in bed with her, I tell myself.

Y

The apartment was in advanced disarray as if nothing had been picked up in the five days or so since I had seen her last. "Don't look," she said. I stood with my back to the room while Barbara made a few minor alterations. "Do you know what I've been doing?" she said. "I'm writing an adult novel about modern marriage."

She took a folded up sheet of paper from her purse and read out loud the most recent version, she said, of the opening sentence. "When Hilda Karpatsky discovered one morning that she was in love with her husband's best friend, she felt herself standing on a narrow precipice on which a move in any direction was to risk disaster."

I hadn't sat down, had accepted a glass of white wine, was moving about the living room looking for an uncluttered place to sit when the phone rang.

Barbara gave me a complicit look, let the ringing play itself out. The phone persisted beyond Barbara's will to ignore it. "It might be important," she said. She took the call in the bedroom. "I was in the shower," I heard her say, then she lowered her voice.

When she returned ten minutes later to the living room, she had a pained smile on her face, the ironic look of someone who feels wrongfully punished. "Guess who?" she said.

I shook my head, could imagine. "Peter."

"That was Adrienne," she said. "She wanted to know if you were here."

I could feel my face burning.

"I don't know how I get into these situations," Barbara said. "Adrienne's my friend too."

"Did you say I was here?"

"Yuri, the question really took me by surprise. I didn't tell her, but I hesitated before I answered. She had to know I was lying."

"I didn't know I was going to be here," I said. "How could Adrienne know?"

"She must have a detective following you. That's all I need now is to get named correspondent in a divorce suit."

"There's no detective," I insisted, though I wondered.

I imagined someone, some callow detective's assistant with a scruffy beard, shadowing me. Had he followed me to the lawyer's office?

Hysteria is seductive. I remember holding her tightly by the shoulders to calm her. When I let go (after how long? We were both possessed.) she punched me in the chest, in the heart it seemed. I couldn't catch my breath and it panicked me. She threw her arms around me, said she was sorry, really sorry. I felt suffocated and pushed her away to free myself. She bumped into something—the arm of a chair—and disabled her back. "Please leave," she said, bent over like an old woman. "You don't live here."

I saw my inflamed face in the mirror as I stepped into the hall. It was the madman in the mirror who shadowed me as I walked quickly home to Adrienne and Rebecca though the half-lit, night world streets.

R

When I closed my eyes, I could see the bugs marching up the stairs. They were the color, these bugs, of dark stairs. It was the way they got at you without being seen.

The bed was feeling buggy near my right foot. I stayed very very still. I was thinking, Turn on the light, Rebecca. I was thinking, Here goes. I'm turning on the light. I'll get out of bed and turn on the light.

A

I've felt nothing toward Yuri for the longest time—neither love nor hate (each had its season). Then I wake during the night and I watch Yuri sleeping on his side facing away from me and I feel this surge of affection for him. (It is the day after I saw C in the street with the red-headed waitress.) I put my hand out and touch his arm as if I were a blind person reading braille. I stroke his arm with the tips of my fingers. He mumbles something that might be a name. (Who are you dreaming of, Yuri?)

He has his back to me and I lay against him front to back, my arms like a sash around his waist. (I am bewitched.) Now he stirs. He takes a long time to wake, his body flaming with sleep. We fit together like two replicas of the same model.

I am kissing his ear. Pressing my mouth against his ear. Sucking his ear. He moans, then reaches behind him to touch my leg. "What is this?" he asks in ironic complaint.

I move my hand along his arms, caress his arms. He doesn't move. The touching, the repeated touching, excites me. "What do you want, baby," I say. "Do you want to make love?"

"Okay," he says, his voice thick. He turns around in a kind of retarded motion (it is the slowest I have ever seen you move) to look at me. It is as though it is not real to him.

"We don't have to," I say.

He moves himself on top of me and kisses me without tenderness or affection. "I don't know if I want you," he says.

"I think you do," I say. "I think you love me." (I don't know why I said that.) "Well, should I put my diaphragm in?"

173

I take his silence for assent, but when he moves off me, I can't get up. I feel weak and lazy. I feel a kind of sensuous paralysis. "Do you want to get it for me?" I ask him.

"I want nothing from you," he says in a hoarse voice. (The lie detector between your legs refutes your denial.)

"I'll leave you alone if that's what you want," I say. I remove my hand. I move all the way over to my side of the bed.

It is interesting what one thinks when one is prepared to think of nothing. I am free associating. I remember sitting next to Yuri in the movies (it was before everything) and wanting to be touched by him. I tried to will him to make the first move. I concentrated on making it happen. His arm brushed mine on the armrest we shared. The movie (it comes back to me) was an Italian film of "The Stranger." I ran my finger along the back of his hand, then withdrew my hand. He reached over and took it back (he took my hand) and kissed the palm.

"If you want to make love, I'm still in the mood," I say.

"I don't want to make love to you," he says. "It's only my prick that's interested."

"Then why don't you fuck me?"

"What I'd like to do is go down on you," he says.

I resist offering an interpretation. (I do not say your intent is hostile.) I have been tormented my whole life by double consciousness. I watch myself feeling shy and somewhat (this surprises me) threatened by him, not answering because I want him to know what I am feeling without being told. I want him to be in touch with me.

He will later claim that I was testing him, but what do I need to prove after all these years together that I don't already know?

Y

Adrienne was at the dinner table, lingering over coffee when I came in. Rebecca was somewhere else.

"We waited for you as long as we could," Adrienne said as if the opening line of a memorized speech.

I went upstairs to visit Rebecca, wondered why she hadn't come down to greet me when she heard me come in. Her door was closed and I knocked. "It's daddy," I said.

"Mommy said you weren't coming home till late," she said. She was lying on her bed fully dressed, facing the wall.

I sat down on the edge of her bed. "Did you have a bad day, sweetheart?"

"I had a good day," she said. "It's you who had a bad day. If you're getting a divorce, I don't want to talk to you again."

I was caught between wanting to apologize for letting things come apart and wanting to insist on my innocence and good faith against charges I hadn't heard. "What did mommy say to you?" I asked.

"You'll have to ask her yourself," she said, then she turned around to look at me. "She said that you both loved me, but that you were not happy with each other."

She let me hug her for a minute or two, then pulled away. "I'm still angry with you," she said.

"Becca, I want you to know," I said, "that I'm doing everything I can to save this marriage. I promise you that." "Daddy, I don't know how to break this to you," she said. "I want to be by myself. Okay?"

"You're beginning to sound like your mother," I said.

"Well, she's her mother's daughter," Adrienne said. She was standing in the doorway of Rebecca's room.

"I thought this was a private conversation," I said. Rebecca groaned. "Daddy!" she said.

Adrienne, I noticed, was wearing an inappropriately beatific smile. "The two of you looked so sweet together, I couldn't resist coming over," she said.

"We were talking about divorce," I said.

R

It's morning and I am in bed. My father is shaving away in the bathroom. The motor of his electric razor is like a speeding heartbeat.

My mother says at breakfast she is afraid of roaches not for themselves but for the disease they spread. What disease is that? my father says.

I ask my father if he saw anything on the basement steps. He says, That's a funny question, Becca. Was there something I was supposed to see.

I don't say what. I am a mysterious person.

B follows me to school. Does she know who I am? What have I done that's so bad she has to follow me?

I have an earache at school and ask the teacher if I can go home. They call my mother from the assistant principal's office but no one answers the phone. I hold my head in my hands.

Later Ms. Dickstein, the assistant principal, reaches my mother and I go home. Where were you? I say to her. I shout at her. I am so mad. Where were you?

A

(I've never completely understood how feelings turn themselves around without warning.) His head perches over me, hesitates (he is waiting for permission), then drops into my unmade lap. I may or may not have gripped him by the short hairs at the back of the neck. I've been told by Yuri (it's not something I mean to dispute here) that I suffer from selective amnesia. (Even when I lie it is my way of telling the truth,)

This is what I remember. My hand is at the back of his head. I remember feeling the thickness of his knotted hair. I remember feeling that what I want doesn't matter (my feelings don't matter) to Yuri.

There is no premeditation to what I do. I am open to whatever comes next. (He doesn't know his place, I say to myself.) I am thinking just that as I pull his head away. (I felt assaulted. I didn't want to be in your debt.) "That's not what I want," I say.

"You hurt me," he says. A giggle escapes from me. (I feel myself trembling.) He is furious.

I cover my face with my arms. "Don't you dare," I say. I close my eyes and wait.

Y

"I think it's nice that you can have talks with your father," said my saintly wife. "When I was your age, Bec, I couldn't talk to your father... I mean my stepfather. Spencer." The voice unutterably sweet, distant, hidden.

Rebecca took my hand and I sensed—it was too dark in the room to know for sure—that she was also holding her mother's hand. She was connecting us. I felt the connection with such intensity it frightened me.

When I left Rebecca's room—Adrienne stayed on with her, I had things to do, felt compelled to move on—I experienced a sense of relief. There was more going on in that room than I could stand for long.

Who was I to be so unforgiving? I thought.

Later that night, I sought Adrienne out in the bedroom, where she sat propped up on pillows with her open sketchbook like a napkin in her lap. "You were very sweet tonight," I said.

An awkward silence followed. Adrienne seemed about

to say something, though withheld whatever it was. A vague smile flickered across her face. "What?" I said.

"I felt better about you tonight," she whispered. "I looked at you with Rebecca and I thought, Well I like him really. I do like you, Yuri. ... Sometimes." She laughed to conciliate the "sometimes".

"If you like me, why do we live like this?" I asked.

She laughed giddily. "I don't know," she said.

I imagined moving into the bed with her, sliding under the covers, tracing the inside of her thigh with my tongue.

"I like you best at a distance," she said as if she had read my thoughts. "When you're next to me, I want to get away."

"Take off," I said under my breath. "I don't want you."

She turned her head away. "That's your problem," she said.

"Look at me, for God's sake." I turned her head to face me, held her face. "I'm Yuri," I said. "I'm the man you chose to marry. I'm the man you love."

"I see you, Yuri," she said in a singsong voice. Then she closed her eyes. "I don't have to see you if I don't want to."

"I don't think you know who I am," I said. "I'm not the father who deserted you. I'm not the stepfather who patted your teenaged ass."

She giggled. "Don't be an asshole," she said. "Is this your idea of shock therapy? You really think I'm crazy, don't you?" She opened her eyes.

"Who am I, Adrienne?" I brought my face closer, posed for the picture she might take of me. I waited with a sense of expectation for her verdict. "I want an answer," I said. "I'm not going to answer you," she said.

When I woke in the early morning, Adrienne was pressed against me from behind, her arms around me. She was so close she seemed to have moved under my skin.

A

I feel the blow (my eyes are closed), though he swears he hasn't touched me. He bashes the pillow with his fist so close to my head that I feel the blow's menace. My head is spinning. (Did you only mean to frighten me, Yuri? That's violence too.) I know I've been hurt.

I knew I had been hurt. I was in shock. My body was shaking— the fear like sexual feelings. No one has ever treated me this way, I said to myself in outrage. No one. At the same time, it was all terribly familiar. (Yuri is, is not, apologizing.) This is what I remembered. I turned away to let the memory play itself out.

I was twelve or thirteen and my step-father had gotten furious at me for being "sassy" to him. (He meant "sexy," though he didn't know that was what he meant.) "You're not too old, young lady, to take over my knee," he said. I ran into the bathroom and locked the door, or thought I had it locked, recalled my fingers turning the latch. For whatever reason, the door didn't lock (you would say, Yuri, that I had meant it not to), though I didn't realize that until later when Spencer forced his way in.

I stood in the bathtub, the shower curtain wrapped around me like a second skin. "Open the door, you," he said. My hands were sweating and I blotted them against my breasts. I had the illusion that I was bleeding, that my period had started (I had only recently turned that corner) before it was due. "Go away," I whispered into the curtain. Though I assumed the door was locked, I felt vulnerable to him.

He kept knocking and knocking (beating on the door with his fist) and then as if he had worn it out, the door came open. I knew I was in for it then. He didn't come in right away, which heightened the terror I was feeling. (Where was my mother when this was happening, why was she letting it happen?)

"When you hide in the bathroom, darlin," he said with a harsh laugh, "you'll have to remember to lock the old door."

"Go to hell," I muttered. (It might have been something worse.)

"What did you say?" he asked in a bullying voice. "What was that, darlin?"

I repeated it for him, mumbled the offensive words, wrapped in my plastic sheath, the bleeding (I felt) a disfiguring punishment for my badness. "Fuck off, you bastard." I don't really know what I said or what he imagined he heard. Whatever, it provoked him to enter. Gave him the excuse he was looking for all along.

He did this strange thing next: he latched the door behind him. He stood there silently (I imagined him a step away from the tub), his disfigured silhouette looming over me. His breathing was like the sound of a furnace just turning on. It came in rushes. I shut my eyes. He stayed there without doing anything for what seemed like a long time.

I anticipated that at any moment he would rip the shower curtain from me. And do what? He would do something so awful (I couldn't imagine what it would be) that I would never be able to forgive him.

And yet I was fully clothed. I was wearing a yellow sundress, which I thought of as babyish for my age. I was reluctant to cry out. I was talking to myself under my breath, "I promise I'll be good if you go away," but not saying it so he could hear it, not willing to give him the least satisfaction. I didn't know about ambivalence then. I was conscious of wishing him away. Some part of me must have believed that I deserved whatever punishment Spencer was there to give out. I was a sassy girl, after all. I had sexual feelings. I had a reputation for being wild. His breathing seemed like a kind of communication. Why couldn't he catch his breath, what was he asking of me in this wordless voice? I knew even then, though it was not conscious knowledge, that the breathing was a kind of love message. Spencer never expressed feelings directly, not feelings of affection or tenderness. The words he might have spoken had fragmented into broken sounds, the machinery of wheeze and death and hate (and love too, I believe) and a passion for connection he surely didn't want to face.

My eyes opened. They had been closed for what seemed like an hour, delusory protection against being discovered. That he hadn't moved for a long time, that he seemed to be affixed to whatever spot he had taken as his own, was no assurance that he wouldn't come at me when he was good and ready. I never stopped hoping that he would leave, that he would decide I had been punished enough. I dug my nails into my arm. My breathing seemed to increase in volume (we made a kind of music together) while I wanted nothing more than to disappear into mute repentance.

He came at me, attacked me. He tore the curtain away, tore at it with both hands, the plastic tearing, curtain rings clattering into the tub. I felt it was me and not the curtain that was being torn and dismantled. It was a surprise to discover afterward that I was essentially unharmed. A purple bruise on my arm was all I took away from his assault. I do remember him slapping me across the face, though that may have been another time. And then he exposed himself (I've not mentioned this to you) and sidled out. When it was over, when he left me, I promised myself that I would never forgive him. (You are saying, I'm sorry, I'm sorry, I'm sorry. It's too late for that.) I can forgive him now.

Twelve

Separate Hours: A Case Study

Adrienne and Yuri Tipton, both psychotherapists with analytic training, had been married for twelve years when their relationship began to go sour. They are both psychotherapists, though of different theoretical persuasion—Adrienne a Laingian and Yuri an eclectic Freudian. In practice, the distinction was not as exceptional as it seemed in theory. According to the available evidence (eg. interviews with former and current patients), their therapeutic methods were virtually mirror images of one another. If their techniques were similar, they nevertheless had different, really opposing personal styles. Yuri's performance with patients was nearer (this an aspect of trying to become what he is not) to Adrienne's theories than to his own. He was, in fact, a more intuitive one to one therapist than Adrienne, who was herself so intuitive in her day to day life she felt the necessity of methodological constraints in her practice. Consequently, her performance as therapist was considerably more conservative, more predetermined so to speak, than her idea of the therapist's ideal role. Adrienne and Yuri had discussed their positions so often, each taking the most uncompromising stance for the sake of argument, that it had made possible unacknowledged accommodation to the other's position.

Adrienne had believed for a long time, not a duration readily circumscribed, that Yuri was better at what they both did than she. She admired him, though kept from him the secret of her admiration. All marriages rely to a greater or lesser extent on the fantasy each partner has created of the other. In rare circumstances, the reality and the fantasy come together like shadows of one another. The lover never sees clearly; the light is always in his eyes. Adrienne envied Yuri's apparent ease of performance, his persistent sense of sureness even in areas of marked ambiguity. So she appropriated him, took on his presumed qualities like a second skin. But the Yuri she appropriated was an imaginary figure, a fantasy figure wiser and more potent than the original. If Adrienne felt herself on safe ground by appropriating her fantasy of Yuri (she wanted only to be perfect), she also resented the obligation such mimicry implied. There was small satisfaction in being her husband's lesser self, particularly when she sensed (their competitiveness was clearly a factor) that she was ready to out-distance him.

As her dissatisfaction grew, she became aware that she was connected to Yuri to an intolerable degree. It was as if she had no edges, no beginning or end. It was only natural that she pull away, and so she gradually revised her fantasy of Yuri. In the new light she brought to bear, Yuri had more failings than she could, while honoring herself, readily tolerate. Disappointment was everywhere. The way to save herself was to fall in love elsewhere.

This is all surmise, a persuasive conjecture based on incomplete evidence.

As Adrienne moved away from him, Yuri felt compelled to move closer to keep things as they were. He pursued the ghost of Adrienne's devotion. Such behavior engendered contempt. It became clear to Adrienne that she had subordinated herself to a man who was unworthy of her self-denial. As she saw it, Yuri had pretended to be something he was not, had offered himself to her as perfect. That made her angry. Such deception, which was how she experienced Yuri's failure to live up to her idealized version of him, was unforgiveable.

For his part, Yuri suffered the abruptness of her disaffection, misunderstood its nature and sought vainly (I use the word in its double sense) to make amends. He looked for ways to please her, reinvented himself to satisfy what he imagined she wanted. Once the process of her disillusionment reached a certain momentum, however, there was no reversing it. His attempts at accommodation only fueled her disaffection. Every gesture he made, in the light of her angry disappointment, was interpreted against him.

What did Adrienne hope to gain from the course of this behavior? Nothing really. Everything. A more fully developed sense of self. There were no petty self-interested motives or none that she allowed to take hold of her consciousness. Her behavior was governed by compulsion and ambivalence. She wanted to get away from Yuri and she wanted to have him at hand. She wanted never to see him again and to know that she could count on him when she needed him. What she really wanted was to live out her real destiny (as opposed to the false one as Yuri's other self), the map of which was buried, she sensed, in embryonic form in her psyche.

So she made Yuri into a version of her first husband, Ralph. It was an exchange of one fantasy for another. Yuri was no longer an enhanced version of the father who left her, but had become instead a combination of her mother and stepfather—the uncaring parent. His imperfections magnified under her glance. Each time she thought herself free of Yuri, she would look at the suffering victim, which is how she experienced him, and feel a tug of affection. The man depended on her—how could she possibly leave him? The process fed on itself. Such feelings of bondage oppressed her, made her want to escape Yuri all the more. She couldn't nurture indefinitely this man she no longer loved. She had a newly discovered separate life of her own that clearly had to have priority. She felt her situation was unique, though she knew a number of women, a few of whom had been patients, who had suddenly found themselves out of love with husbands they had once adored. She made common cause with them. Their examples gave her courage.

Yuri was unwilling to believe that Adrienne had stopped loving him, perceived her changed behavior as a form of displacement, a passing phase. He hated her for betraying him, but he also wanted to forgive her. If she was appropriately regretful, he was willing to forgive everything. Which is also to say he could forgive nothing. His sole aim was some kind of restitution—the way it was, the way it had always been. What sustained him was the fantasy that he had behaved well in the face of arbitrary cruelty.

They went on this way for a year, Yuri struggling to regain his place, alternately wooing and accusing, Adrienne drawing away from him, reimagining herself as a woman who needed no one but herself. Yuri glimmered in the distance of her imagination like a spectral image. Only his faults had presence for her. He took space in her life and at the same time he was bodiless—virtually invisible to her. And she knew he wanted her back, wanted things as they were, though he took pains to deny it. His wanting her back sustained her in her rejection of him.

They lived together this way in poised disequilibrium, in a state of unarmed warfare, for more than a year, for almost two years. Their professional lives went on as before. They continued to share the basement office of their westside brownstone for therapy sessions, though complained to friends— it was rare that they talked openly to each other— of the difficulties of such an arrangement. Occasionally, they made appointments to see patients at the same time, a way of unacknowledging the other. The more estranged they became, the harder it was to maintain the arrangement of separate hours.

The new fantasy of their marriage required a new set of gestures. Both were compelled to prove (against the evidence of their feelings) that they were not dependent on the other. Yuri went to London for ten days to a conference on the use of computer technology in psychotherapeutic treatment. He delivered a paper that was well received, had a brief affair with a woman who treated behavioral disorders with massive doses of vitamins, felt more positive about himself. Adrienne had been invited to the same conference but had declined the invitation, saying next time it was her turn. That remark might be seen as evidence that she harbored the illusion that they would go on this way forever.

When Yuri returned from London he sensed that Adrienne was pleased to see him and he made some advances toward her (he thought of it as opening new lines of communication) that got him nowhere. She suffered his absence, though took no pleasure in his return. Her perception (her fantasy) of the man who came back to her was different from her perception of the man she had missed. Things remained as they had been.

Adrienne avoided Yuri except at dinner, usually stayed upstairs when he was down or downstairs when he was up. It was a regimen of denial. Sometimes they met on the stairs to (and from) their office, surprised that the other was still around. In private, they mourned each other's absence.

Their ten year old daughter Rebecca, an exceptionally bright and sensitive child, took on the role of parent in the face of her mother and father's abdication of adult responsibility. "Why don't you spend more time with daddy?" she'd say to Adrienne. "I don't mind staying with Sandy (her baby sitter) if you guys want to go out together."

She would say to her father, "The trouble with you, Daddy, is that you give up too easily. Mommy likes you a lot more than you think."

Yuri and Adrienne heard what they wanted to hear, took justification where none was offered.

It was a problematic situation, the way they lived, particularly for Yuri who was perceived as the rejected one. Friends wondered how he could continue to live in the same house with someone who made him feel unwanted. Yuri took solace in knowing (or believing he knew) that matters at home were not as terrible as outsiders imagined them to be.

For a while, Rebecca had trouble getting to sleep at night, had unadmitted fears concerning abandonment.

Yuri began to see women outside his marriage, rarely staying longer than three months with the same one. The affairs had a certain pattern: intense beginnings, flights of passion, followed by disappointment and withdrawal. Nothing sustained itself, which troubled Yuri, his feelings rarely the same from day to day, love visiting briefly like mail sent to the wrong address. He perceived himself as still married to Adrienne, as permanently married to her. A vulnerability he could not remember having known before kept him constant company.

His longest involvement during this period was with a former patient (a stand-in in his fantasy for the Adrienne of fifteen years back), an erotic commitment that held Yuri almost as intensely as his collapsing marriage. He had lost the Adrienne-who-was-no-longer-Adrienne and taken in her place the more-real-than-real- Adrienne.

Adrienne wanted no one for a while, wanted only her own company after her love affair with a former patient ended. She could not forgive Yuri for letting her treat him as badly as she had. She could not go back to what had been. That much was relatively clear. That more had come to her meant that more was still to come. She expected her lover to return to her, not literally perhaps (she had mostly given up that false hope), but what she had with him (the fantasy of), the flowering of some deeper, more creative self she expected would return. While she waited for the new life that awaited her, she tested her attractiveness in a few relationships with other men, men who were safe, who didn't matter, passionless dances. It was a period of restoration for her.

They went on like this for longer than anyone who knew them imagined possible. Observers tended to think that it was Yuri's tenacity that kept them together, his refusal to let go. He had decided apparently to refuse defeat, to outwait Adrienne's disaffection. Tenacity had gotten him everything he wanted so far and his faith in his own persuasive powers was outsized. Perhaps he loved Adrienne so much he was willing to put up with anything to keep her. Perhaps it was a mix of dependence and love, a confusion of the two. Adrienne appeared to assume, had said as much in confidence to several friends, that Yuri couldn't manage without her. Such statements are readily decoded. The person who thinks himself (herself) the object of dependency tends also to be dependent.

When Yuri was much younger—it was just after he had completed medical school and gone into the service—he fell in love with a southern woman, someone he met in Charlottesville when on leave from the Air Force. The woman, a former child actress, swore that she would wait for him, though she ultimately married someone else. When he was released from the Air Force, Yuri rented a house across the bay from where the woman, no longer performing, lived with her husband and child. He fantasized that once she saw him again she would remember that she had loved him. A year after this period of vigil, Yuri went into analysis and decided to become an analyst himself.

They were in a deadlock, Yuri waiting for Adrienne to return to him, Adrienne acting as if he weren't there, for two years, almost three.

Just when their estranged life together seemed to have achieved a certain stability, Yuri told Adrienne that he wanted a divorce. The news, it appears (which is not surprising), surprised her. For the first time in years, she was not in control of the situation. She may even have suffered feelings of rejection, her prerogatives denied her. Still, a divorce was what she imagined herself wanting, what she had been moving (in place) toward, and she agreed in principle with his decision.

So Yuri left Adrienne, sublet the apartment of a friend, also a therapist, which was initially a relief to both of them. They talked on the phone almost every day, exchanged anecdotes (reconstituted former intimacy), made arrangements for passing Rebecca between them.

Now that we're separated, Adrienne said, I feel close to you again. I feel that we can be real friends. She told Yuri about a man she had been seeing, described some of the problems of the relationship.

I really don't want to talk to you, Yuri said. I don't want you to call me any more.

Adrienne felt justified at having broken with him (Yuri was graceless and unreliable), though she also suffered feelings of deprivation. It was as if something that was rightfully hers was being denied her. The next time she called it was concerning the roof of the house that needed, according to the roofer she had consulted, extensive repair. Was the roofer trustworthy? Yuri asked. Adrienne took offense at the question, said she was every bit as competent in dealing with such matters as he was. Yuri didn't argue the issue—his principal concern was to get off the phone—said to go ahead and have the job done if it needs to be done.

Don't you think I should get a few other estimates? asked Adrienne. It's really a lot of money.

Then get some other estimates, said Yuri.

I really don't think we're going to find anyone cheaper than Mr. Pustulli, said Adrienne.

Then use Pustulli, said Yuri. I don't have any problem with that.

I just want to make sure it's all right with you, she said, before I go ahead with it. What have you been doing?

Yuri said he couldn't talk, was on his way out.

She too was busy, she said. She had a new patient coming in a few minutes.

Adrienne was disappointed that they couldn't be friends, had difficulty sympathizing with Yuri's apparent bitterness. It had been her fantasy that they would be better friends than ever once they were separated. As she saw it, Yuri's need to avoid her was *his* problem, something he would eventually work through. For her part, she continued to think a friendship between them was not impossible.

Their lives went on much as before except that they no longer shared the same house or, after Yuri found another space, the same therapy office in the same house. Giving up the shared therapy space was a significant step in their coming apart. Yuri, as mentioned, went through a period of intense sexual activity, wanting both contact and distance, an intimacy that made no demands. He tended to be dour during this period, to seem to be in mourning, to lose weight. He looked as if sleep had become as much a stranger as Adrienne. He wanted, he told his therapist, to fuck himself into unconsciousness.

Adrienne moved in the other direction, became increasingly private, rarely went out in the evenings, worked on her drawings, devoted herself to her daughter. Her health seemed fragile—symptoms of illness plagued her—though nothing specific was determined. She went into the hospital for three days to take a battery of tests. Apart from occasional depression and her anxieties about illness, she felt an ease to her post-married life she couldn't remember having known before. She asked Yuri to drive her to the hospital and, though he grumbled about it, acted as if he were put upon, he did. He also took her back when the tests were completed, insisted on the prerogative, and Adrienne was touched by what she took to be his concern. They held on by reestablishing in their post-marriage some of the ambience of their pre-marriage.

Once she separated from Yuri, Adrienne's obsession with the lover who had rejected her disappeared. For a long time she had ached to see him, had felt his loss like an unhealed wound from childhood. One morning, exactly a week after Yuri's departure, it was gone and she was free of that particular ache, that particular knowledge of loss forever.

Yuri's anger with Adrienne persisted. Whenever he thought of her he dredged up some horror scene from the last years of their marriage. This was a period in which he fell in and out of love almost as often as the weather changed. He thought he wanted to live with a woman again, perhaps with Helena Paar, whom he had just discovered, but he was wary of rushing into anything long term, distrusted his feelings which showed themselves to be untrustworthy. His life was frantic, he seemed to believe, overburdened with commitments. There was little ease, not enough love. He wanted some kind of sexual contact with every attractive woman who crossed his path and risked, on more than one occasion, making a fool of himself. And sometimes all he wanted to do was suck breasts or cunts or be sucked on himself. He couldn't get enough and yet when he had it, had had it, was having it, he longed to escape the demands of pleasure. The life he envisioned for himself was one where commitment to work took priority over everything else. He wanted, while behaving as a child, to think of himself as a serious man.

One day, his friend Barbara, whom he visited Tuesday nights, told Yuri that her husband had asked if he could come back. Her husband Peter had talked about their having another child, something he had adamantly opposed for years. She wanted Yuri's advise, she said, was in need of some wisdom.

You've already decided to take him back, Yuri said, playing the part she had assigned him.

Barbara denied it with some vehemence, though she acknowledged later in the discussion that it was the best offer

SEPARATE HOURS

she had had, meaning apparently that she had none from
Yuri. They put their arms around each other then self-
consciously drew back. It embarrassed Yuri that he had once
slept with his friend Peter's estranged wife. Such behavior
was at odds with the idea he had of himself as a moral man.
Barbara asked if he would remain her friend and, without
irony or without the appearance of irony, Yuri asserted that
he couldn't imagine it otherwise.

When Yuri moved in with Helena—a woman Adrienne didn't know, had never met—Adrienne was secretly
furious with him. She told everyone how pleased she was for
Yuri, though at least on one occasion when she had been
drinking rather heavily she made mildly disparaging remarks
about Helena's intelligence. At other times, she spoke gener-
ously about them both. If her behavior during this period
resembled jealousy, it was probably also a relief to her that
Yuri was no longer her responsibility. It was a time of
unburdening for her, a freeing herself from what she thought
of as false obligations. She cut down on her practice, showed
her drawings (she had done no new ones in a year) to an art
dealer she had dated on two or three occasions, talked of
having an exhibition. The tests she took could find nothing
wrong, but she suffered, she believed, from some inexorable
malady.

One day when Yuri came to the house to return
Rebecca—the child lived alternate weeks with each parent—
Adrienne, who usually kept out of sight, appeared at the
door. She was extremely charming, almost desperately so.
Yuri was reminded of their early days together when he was
married to Patricia and she to Ralph. Adrienne suggested
that they go out for a drink some evening. There was
something important she wanted to discuss with him. She
spoke the word "important" as if it were in italics. Yuri
hesitated—it was his recent role to hesitate whenever she
asked something of him—before saying he didn't see why
not. (The specific language is important to understanding

193

what he meant.) His answer confused her, she said. Was he willing to have a drink with her or not?

Yuri picked her up at the house one night the next week after Rebecca was asleep. They didn't want to go to a local bar—no one was supposed to know about the casual drink they were having together—so they drove out of the city to an inn they had been to before they were married, a place called the Libertyville Canal House. Nothing was said on the drive out about the occasion for this meeting. They talked about the profession they shared in common in a way that was reminiscent of old times together, argued about methods and diagnoses, talked about books read.

Our separation has improved you, Adrienne says in response to one of Yuri's remarks.

In what way? Yuri wants to know.

Just that, Adrienne says. You haven't noticed that I'm wearing the scarf you gave me on our tenth anniversary.

Yuri tells her of an article he has been writing about children of divorced parents.

After dinner at the inn—they have mussels and roast duck and black forest cake for dessert—they decide it is too late to drive back and they take a room for the night. The availability of a room at the Canal House, which is usually booked a month in advance, seems an inescapable omen. Adrienne calls the sitter and makes arrangements with her to stay overnight with Rebecca. Yuri calls Helena to say he will not be back until the next morning. She doesn't ask why and he doesn't volunteer a reason, having none to give, no acceptable excuse. He doesn't want to lie. He has reached a point in his life where he avoids lying whenever possible.

The phone call to Helena depresses Yuri. On his guard, as if some moral arbiter were watching him from above, he imagines he will refuse Adrienne when the time comes. In his fantasy he has already told her it's not going to happen, but when they climb into bed rejecting her is not his first priority.

In bed, after love, he says in a brusque voice, surprised at the tenderness he feels, Is this the important thing you wanted to talk about?

She gives him back his feigned indifference. You're not as funny as you used to be, she says. I woke up the other morning and I remembered how funny you were when we first met. I remembered liking you and I wanted to see if it was real or some nostalgic illusion.

It's all illusion, Yuri says. and its all real.

How smart you are, she says, only partially mocking him. She sits propped up on the narrow bed—it is no more than three- quarter's size—with an arm around his shoulders. —Why did you go along with me? You knew what was going to happen.

I didn't know, he says. I knew and I didn't know. Is that an evasion? It's possible that I was testing my feelings.

You still don't say what you feel, she says.

You throw me over, he says, and now you want me to tell you that I never stopped being in love with you. You're as presumptuous as ever.

I haven't heard anyone say "throw me over" since I was a teenager, Yuri. (She presses her face to his.) I was hoping, I know this sounds silly after all this, that we could still be friends. I've always been fond of you. That's true. There's something about you that makes no sense to me that I like to have around.

It is two in the morning and Yuri, apparently disturbed at the turn of the conversation, suggests they go to sleep.

I don't feel at all sleepy, she says. How can you think of going to sleep? I told you what I was feeling. You have to say something. It's called conversation.

Or transactional therapy, he says. I'm feeling good at this moment, but I know I'm going to hate myself for having done this. After all the shit I've taken from you, you think I'll come running whenever you call.

Do I think that? Adrienne says. I don't know that that's

195

what I think. And what about all the shit I've taken from you? ...Do you love Helena?

The question takes him by surprise. He turns away from her, delays his answer, says Yes.

She turns away from him onto her side, punishes him with distance.

He puts his hand on her back between her shoulder blades, falls asleep touching the hollow of her back. He imagines himself saying, You too, though the words are never spoken. He wakes to find her hugging him.

She whispers, Yuri, if I let myself feel anything for you, I would have never been able to "throw you over". I had to get free. I was suffocating.

But what about me? he says. Are you the only one who has feelings?

Honey, I couldn't tell you then, she says. Try to look at it from my viewpoint. Okay?

I've done too much of that, he says.

Have you? Have you? she says. She is playful, climbs on top of him and pins his arms to his sides. He lies passively for a minute or so, wearing her like a blanket, then he lifts his arms. They wrestle, Adrienne intent on getting her way, intent on holding him down. It is a serious struggle in the guise of play.

It is cold in the room. Adrienne's breath steams. You've had your way long enough, he says, rolling her over abruptly, pinning her down with his weight.

Adrienne absorbs his pressure as if it were her will to have him there. It is her victory, she tells herself.

I shower when I get out of bed, dress myself in yesterday's clothes. A kind of inertia has settled over me, which I make an effort to resist. I ask Adrienne when she has to be back and she doesn't answer, has slipped back into sleep. I think of waking her, but decide against it—she is like a child when she sleeps—and I go out for a walk to pass the time. It is a luxury to walk in the country on a cool June morning. I walk for about twenty minutes until I arrive at a cluster of shops that calls itself a town. There is nothing I want—even so I have brought no money—and I turn back, impatient with the slowness of the day.

Adrienne is dressed and ready to leave when I get back to the room. Where were you? she says in an aggrieved voice. I have to get back for Rebecca. You know that.

I remind her that she had been the one who had fallen asleep. She insists that she was awake, that she heard me open and close the door.

You could have let me know, I say.

Oh Yuri! You knew I was awake.

I'm not going to deal with that, I say. The last thing I want is to have a fight with you now.

The last thing I want, sweetheart, is to have a fight with you, Yuri says.

Oh, Yuri, I say, putting my arms around him, kicking him playfully, you never want to fight.

On the trip back, I tell Yuri a story that I think will amuse him. I have a new patient, a woman about my own age, who is fixed on me in this strange way. Last week when she missed a period, the woman accused me of being responsible for her pregnancy. — Do you think it's some kind of transference? I ask him. In no other way does this woman seem psychotic.

She sees your authority as masculine, Yuri says. Are you sure you're not the father?

If you think I'm making this up, I say, you're wrong.

The car is making an odd banging noise and I ask Yuri to stop and see what's wrong.

We go on another ten minutes like this, the noise growing more and more ominous. He will get off at the next exit, Yuri says. We don't get to the next exit. A tire blows (I don't know that at the time) and we go out of control, skid crazily on to the dirt collar. It all happens so quickly there is no time to know how terrified I am. We come to a stop inches from a low metal fence guarding an embankment.

Damn it, Yuri yells. Those are his words of comfort to his passenger. We both get out of the car. Do you have a good spare? I ask him.

He doesn't answer, doesn't open the trunk to look, says something about needing to catch his breath.

If you give me the key to the trunk, I'll change the tire myself, I say.

He walks away from me, stares into the distance. I pick up a stone and throw it at him. His back is to me when I throw this harmless small stone, but he turns in midflight and it catches him in the face just under the right eye. I let out a cry of warning when I see what's going to happen. Then all of a sudden he's tearing after me and I'm running for my life. Bitch, I hear him yell. The entire highway hears him.

At wit's end, I turn and face him (there is no place to go) and we exchange a few punches and kicks and roll around in the dirt. I am afraid he will hurt me and I cry out when a punch to the head produces not stars so much as flashes of lightning. And then he stops. I feel grateful to have survived.

After the fight is over, he opens the trunk of the car. He changes the tire (the spare is minimally usable) while I sit on a rock looking in another direction. Imagining how we must appear to the people in the cars streaming by, I start to laugh.

We have little to say to each other the rest of the trip. I am no longer angry at him, but it is not something I can say. When we stop in front of the house, I am aware of how shy I feel with him. I lean toward him and barely touch his cheek with my lips. It is what I mean. It is all I mean. I don't like to give the wrong impression. Yuri touches my shoulder, says, See you.

See you, I say and hurry out of the car.

I watch Adrienne unlock the door of the house and go inside—"our" house, I am thinking, though of course it is no longer mine—consider saying hello to Rebecca, though drive off. It would only confuse her to know I was with her mother. Anyway, I'll be taking her to my place the day after tomorrow. The radio is on—I don't remember pressing the button—and I listen to David Bowie singing "Absolute Beginners." I have to be at clinic in an hour and I consider stopping off at home to change my clothes. I look at myself in the rearview mirror—my face smeared with dirt, a mean cut below my right eye—and I see there is no way to explain away what happened. I decide to go on and call Helena from my office at the hospital.

They didn't go off again together.

Two years after she split up with Yuri, Adrienne's stepfather died and she took his death harder than anyone anticipated. Yuri's loss no longer seemed to matter. In her revisionist fantasy, her marriage had eroded of its own accord. They could no longer live together (their marriage had become impossible), though when asked why, she was vague about the details. She tended to remember that they were good together at their best, and she blamed Yuri just a little for being impatient with her during a period of emotional crisis in her life.

For Yuri, the night with Adrienne at the inn in upstate New York was a conclusion to the relationship. As an apparent consequence, he felt free of Adrienne and was able to commit himself more fully to Helena, who was in certain unapparent ways like Adrienne (this was Yuri's perception alone), though she was not a therapist but a designer of women's clothes. He no longer hated Adrienne, and he was able to talk to her on the phone, and sometimes in person, without anger or sadness. Eventually he married Helena and they had a child together, a son.

Adrienne did not remarry.

Thirteen

Last Words

Yuri

I have no more to say about my marriage to Adrienne. Peter says, Peter who lives in a state of perpetual undeclared war with Barbara, that divorce is an indicator of success in post-civilized America. He says it self-mockingly because he himself has been close to divorce and has put his marriage back together again as if it were a broken table. It is his theory that people in our milieu break faith with their marriages in pursuit of self-improvement. I don't feel successful in having divorced Adrienne. On the contrary, I see it as a compromise with the demands of romantic

Adrienne

There are times (yes, this is true) that I feel totally at peace as if body and soul had achieved some effortless union. Rebecca and I tend to be easier with each other in Yuri's absence. I am more my own person, more and more my own person. (And yet some things remain the same. I try to please, I am always trying to please.) When I lie in bed in the early morning awaiting the call of the next day, I focus on who I am. Who am I? I am Adrienne French. It is discouraging sometimes to be no one other than oneself. But who else is there? I am all I have. My secret self has become my public persona.

ambition. It is easier to live with Helena. We don't take our emotional pulses every hour; we are not unhappy if we're not happy. We respect each other's otherness. That's a kind of sanity. Adrienne and I, for all our time in therapy, for all our time as therapists confused the boundaries between us. Adrienne was everything to me: lover, wife, daughter, mother, father, closest friend, rival, other self. Our marriage had to be perfect or it was nothing. What I wonder at is not that we came apart but that we survived together as long as we had. Helena and I talk openly with each other, make a point of being honest, but there are certain things I am unable to share with her. Can I tell her that I dream about Adrienne, that I continue to hold conversations with her in my imagination, that when I wake from dreams in the dead hours of the night, I think of Adrienne as my wife? How can I let Helena know that without making her feel betrayed?

I hope that I am not

Yuri and I played house for a while with what appeared to be success. Yes. We were stuck and something had to be done, and I was the one who did it. I confess I did it. I acted (or acted out if you insist) for the both of us. I've always lived on the knife edge of my feelings. I was the first one to do what the other children were afraid to do. I went (I always did) where it was forbidden to go. The bad child is the brave child.

Love is its own betrayal. My late step-father's favorite expression, which Grace and I often mocked (we were such bad girls) is: You can't make an omelet without breaking eggs. My question is: Did I break more eggs than needed to be broken? My answer: The more eggs you break the more substantial the omelet.

I am a more successful therapist for what I've gone through. I've had successes recently with patients who had been judged untreatable by certain esteemed analysts. I have a gift. I am gifted at therapy. It has taken me a giving the wrong impression, that language has not again taken me beyond where I mean to go. I love Helena, and I believe she loves me without having to make more of me than I am. I have not said anything about sex. We Freudians tend to overstate its importance, to see it as the central mystery, the anima of all other pleasures and pains. A delicacy of feeling restrains me here. I find myself hesitant in saying that sex with Helena is one of the major pleasures of this middleaged therapist. It is said. I move on.

Now I come to another admission that for different reasons I have been reluctant to make. Though my life is good, I am not greatly happy, not happy enough of the time. This awareness taunts me. It is as though just behind me, just out of view, something is missing that completes the puzzle. It is a sadness that occupies me even in moments of intense joy.

I am not so blindly romantic as to believe my former wife the cause of this unresolved freefloating grief.

long time to be able to say this.

No tragedy, my life. No one has died of grief or heartbreak. No one has killed herself. (I've had this feeling all my life that I am doomed. That I will die young. Yes, but I am no longer young.)

It is sad to me that Yuri doesn't want to be my friend. (We had been friends in our way for such a long time.) If only for Rebecca's sake such reconciliation makes sense. Maybe Yuri hasn't allowed himself to forgive me. (In time.) Our exchanges are mostly abrupt and businesslike. In my dreams, he is like some relentless figure of vengeance pursuing me. He will never forgive me, never let me go.

Yuri knows what's between us (let him deny it), and what he has with Helena, whatever he thinks it is, is not the same. I have lovers too. (I protest too much. It doesn't matter.)

My art is the most fulfilling thing I have. Some-

I am a rational man who likes to be clear about what he's doing and why he's doing it. It is my life's work after all to make clarity out of confusion. That's the side of me that others value most. The other side is fathomless and dangerous. The other pursues only the elusive and so courts disappointment.

For all that I understand, I understand nothing that matters. I admit that without embarrassment. I go through life blindfolded in an endless tunnel of my own imaginative creation and what I want—that insatiable ache—what I reach out for in the mysterious dark, touches me briefly then slips away into the ether. I have had for the briefest time whatever it is I have lost, and I have somehow let it escape my grasp. It is no wonder that some kind of irremediable illness looms behind me when I turn my head.

times it seems the only thing. My vision. Each time I believe I am through drawing birds, the same elegant erotic studies, I rediscover my subject. Some day I will give up doing therapy, and concentrate (full time) on my art.

Whatever the rumors (such talk echoes), I am not unhappy, I am not depressed or anxious much of the time. I feel I have to announce that to myself and to those who want to pity me. (Pity is just malice in black silk.) This woman, Adrienne is not unhappy with her life. She knows that there is nothing to regret. She knows that love is only one of a number of illusions that dies and never comes back to life. Love died with Yuri; love left us for good. It doesn't matter. (Forgive me, Yuri.) There is no recovery from this illness.